THE MONSOON MURDERS

THE MONSOON MURDERS

Karan Parmanandka

Srishti
PUBLISHERS & DISTRIBUTORS

SRISHTI PUBLISHERS & DISTRIBUTORS
Registered Office: N-16, C.R. Park
New Delhi – 110 019
Corporate Office: 212A, Peacock Lane
Shahpur Jat, New Delhi – 110 049
editorial@srishtipublishers.com

First published by
Srishti Publishers & Distributors in 2016

10 9 8 7 6 5 4 3 2 1

This is a work of fiction. The characters, places, organisations and events described in this book are either a work of the author's imagination or have been used fictitiously. Any resemblance to people, living or dead, places, events or organisations is purely coincidental. The author asserts the moral right to be identified as the author of this work.

The scene on pp. 93-94 is inspired from "One time at the beach" featured in Ingmar Bergman's Swedish movie *Persona* (1966).

This edition is for sale in the Indian subcontinent only.

Printed and bound in India

Dedicated to
those who are,
those who were,
and those who never could be...

Inspired from real life cases.

Prologue

The car rolled into the street that housed his apartment. He looked around for his umbrella, but seemed to have had left it in the office. The rain was gentle and his house was just a short distance from the road. He reckoned he could run the distance, and looked forward to the cup of coffee to warm up his bones. He stepped out of the car, shutting the door behind him.

Just then, he had a feeling of being stared at, like a set of eyes piercing his back. He turned around. Across the road, he could see a glinting black object peeping from a partially constructed building, but the rain made it difficult to make out the barrel of the gun.

Though he could barely see the gun, he clearly felt the sharp sting of the bullet hitting his right shoulder. Instead of ducking for cover, strangely he reached out for his shirt pocket and pulled out his spectacles. He gave a short jerk to spread out his glasses and carefully put them on to get a better look at the wound. “Shoot him again,” K whispered to Debu. This time Debu was more accurate. The bullet pierced through the rain and hit its target right in between the lungs.

He felt his breath being knocked out. It was the wrong time to die, he thought. His job was still unfinished. But at the same time, he was thankful for having been shot in the chest, the only respectful way for a police officer to die.

It is said that when one is fatally hurt, his entire life flashes by. But that did not happen with him. He could only think of two people as he lay there wounded.

The Call

The caller was an unfamiliar voice with a proposal too tempting to resist and too difficult to accept. Roy picked up his watch. It was seven in the morning, more than a day since the murder. He would have to set out immediately if he hoped to make any sense of the crime scene. He noticed the dark clouds only when he stepped out of the building, but figured that he did not have the time to go back for the jacket.

His bike cut through the nippy monsoon air swiftly, but calmly, hoping to make the fifteen minute journey in five. No sooner had the bike turned the street corner that it began to pour. But this wasn't the day for Roy to turn back. He kept up his steady speed, soaking up the rain. Only when he halted at the red light did he wonder back to the call.

"Is it Roy Konte?"

"Yes," Roy had responded, still groggy from sleep.

"Hello. This is Chandra from Fox Capital Pvt Ltd. We have some work for you. Want you to look into the death of one of our employees."

The mention of death jolted Roy out of his snooze. "Well, you see, I don't investigate murders..." he was cut short.

"What makes you suppose that it's a murder? Anyway, we can discuss all that later," Chandra said. "Right now, I ask you to go to straight to his apartment: Evita Building, Hiranandani Township, Flat A1705." Chandra's voice was curt and authoritative, and made Roy dislike him immediately.

"Wait a second. You don't understand....Call me when you are done," he said as he disconnected the call.

Roy sat on his bike, waiting for the light to turn green. He was still unsure about taking the case, but decided to visit the scene before making up his mind. Though Roy hadn't dealt with the banking world, there was hardly anyone in the city who had not heard of Fox Capital – a wealth management powerhouse catering only to the ultra-rich. Whereas most of the finance firms had their offices to the south of the city, Fox Capital was based out of Hiranandani, and had established a niche for itself by catering to the new money.

While Roy was excited at the assignment, he did have a few concerns. Why did Fox Capital want someone other than the police to investigate the matter? Who was Chandra and what was his relation to the firm? But above all, why was he selected for the job?

The Murder

Hiranandani Gardens in suburban Mumbai was an upscale township built at the turn of the century. Home to the nouveau riche, it was a cluster of spacious apartments in an otherwise asphyxiated city. Within Hiranandani, Evita was a newly constructed building and boasted of some of the most luxurious apartments of the township – the kind of building Roy would have no business visiting in ordinary course of his life.

The discreet nature of his job had taught Roy to leave minimum trace of his visits. He entered the building stealthily, trying to muffle the sound of his footsteps within the lavishly laid carpets. But he was unable to avoid the attention of the guard hunched over the register, who looked up at Roy with a questioning glance. Without batting an eyelid, Roy walked up to him and complained of the visitors parking their cars in his allotted space. The guard stood up in attention and assured him that the mistake would not be repeated. Behind the guard, Roy noticed a pair of security cameras staring straight at him, recording all movements to and from the building. Though one could fool the guards, it was going to be difficult for anyone to enter the building undetected.

Roy took the elevator to the seventeenth floor. He saw a couple of gentlemen standing outside the designated apartment with an official air about them. From the angle at which they stood, he was unable to make out their faces, but Roy could smell out a policeman amongst a crowd of thousand and these two certainly fit the bill. They spoke in hushed voices, and made assured movements, confidently conducting their affairs under the authority entrusted by law. The thickly-built middle-aged guy was pouring instructions to the younger fellow, who hurriedly took down notes in his handbook. Roy wanted to avoid meeting anyone from the force, but it would be impossible for him to enter the apartment without their approval.

Roy approached them politely. "Hello officers."

The senior police officer turned towards him. A few moments of surprised silence, quickly followed by a smile, "Look who's here, if not my old friend Roy. What a pleasure to see you," he said.

Even among these morbid surroundings, Roy was pleased to have bumped into Ketkar. In his early fifties, with a pot belly and a lazy personality, Ketkar's smile could have put anyone at ease. But Roy knew that behind this relaxed exterior was a mind who understood crooks, one who knew how to charm criminals into dropping their guard, and then pounce for the kill. Ketkar was one of only a handful of people in the team with whom Roy shared an easy equation. "Great to see you too Ketkar," Roy's voice was more subdued, for he had not forgotten the circumstances under which they'd met last.

Both of them fell quiet for a moment, stealing awkward glances at each other, with Ketkar making the situation even more difficult by trying hard to act like everything was normal. It was Roy who broke the silence. "Sir, I have been asked by someone to investigate the scene," he spoke with the formality that suited the occasion. The couple of pleasantries exchanged were all that this friendship could afford.

Ketkar too fished out his business manners, "Who is your client, if I may ask?"

"Fox Capital. The deceased was in their employment."

If Ketkar was surprised that a nobody like Roy was approached by the savviest of firms on the street, he did well to not let it show. "That is nice. Can I help you in any way?" Ketkar's last sentence had a ring of dismissal about it.

"Nothing particular. Came here just to have a look." Roy was casual about his request, but knew that he was asking for something which would be tough for Ketkar to accommodate.

"I see," Ketkar said thoughtfully. He took out a coin from his pocket and started to toss it about, looking a bit uncomfortable as he did so. From his experience, Roy knew that Ketkar wanted to say something unpleasant but was unsure how to say it. "You do understand it would be difficult for me to allow you into the crime scene, now that you are just a civilian."

Roy understood Ketkar was asking him to leave. He felt a punch in his guts; as though the investigation would be over before it began. "Just a few cursory observations Ketkar, so I can at least decide what I want to do with it. Shouldn't take long, I guess."

Ketkar stopped juggling the coin and threw a hard stare at Roy. "Look Konte, I have never been much of a stickler for rules and I like you, so I will not be rude to you. But, we all have our boundaries, and I cannot allow you to investigate the case."

But on seeing the dejection on Roy's face, and knowing how much this case meant to him, Ketkar allowed himself to be charitable. "Okay, this is what we are going to do," he said. "I will tell you briefly about the case and walk you around the apartment. You are not to touch anything and not ask more than I am willing to tell you. And don't do anything that makes me regret my decision. Deal?"

"You can count on it, sir," Roy said with a smile.

"Great then, let me introduce you to my partner. This is Romil," Ketkar said pointing towards his baby-faced colleague. "He is the new one in the police force and has been assisting me in this investigation."

As Romil tried to extend his hand towards Roy, he dropped the bag that had been slung across his shoulder. Romil bent down to pick his bag, one arm still extended for the handshake, balancing the notebooks with his other. Roy had seen plenty of his type – young graduates, straight out of the academy, eager to please anyone suspected of being important. For a moment Roy wanted to place his arm over Romil's shoulders, walk with him a few paces and tell him to leave this job while he still had his honour intact.

"Hello Romil, no need to get excited," Roy said. "I am no longer a part of the police team."

"I see. Glad to meet you nonetheless," Romil said with relief.

Ketkar walked Roy into the flat, closely followed by Romil. The front door had a name plaque with 'Mr Arun Ruia' etched onto it. The apartment dripped wealth from all corners – a spacious two bedroom affair tastefully done up in an understated shade of beige. The signs of high living had been strewn across the rooms – glistening marble flooring, leather couches and a state of the art home theatre. "A thing of beauty, don't you think?" Ketkar said darting his eyes across the living room. "Look at this carpet here. My feet just sink in when I stand over it like I have been standing on a bed of roses," he said with the excitement of a small kid walking into an amusement park. Roy was aware of Ketkar's weakness for the high life. Though he was a competent officer, Roy knew Ketkar could not afford his daily scotch on just a government officer's salary.

"The deceased's name is Arun Ruia. Forty-one years old, he was the Executive Director for Currency Trading at Fox Capital, which is owned by Jayesh Kumar. Not much is known of Jayesh's past; we only know he established Fox about ten years back and turned it into one of the most respected names on the street. Arun was poached by Jayesh from Systelax about five years back, lured with the promise of a faster career and a fatter bank account. When Arun decided to jump ship, many of the clients handled by Arun at Systelax also switched their accounts to Fox – a trend quite common in this industry.

"And what happened to Systelax?" Roy asked.

"I am not sure, but I haven't heard of them in the recent past," Ketkar said. "Anyway, they had been hit hard by Arun's defection, and must have found it difficult to recover."

Roy scribbled the name of the firm on his notepad. "We conducted detailed interviews with the office folks," Ketkar continued, "and by all accounts, it appears that Arun was good at his job. Even then, his cut throat attitude and often rude behaviour meant there were a whole bunch of people who felt they were rubbed the wrong way by him at some point or the other. To make matters worse, post the financial crisis restructuring, the company decided to shed some flab and fired half of the staff. I don't know the inside story, but the perception in the company is that while Jayesh wanted to stick it out and carry everyone around, Arun was in favour of culling the under performers. Arun had personally handed out the pink slips, which made him less popular than ever. In fact, at one point, we even had a promising suspect from among the employees at the firm, but eventually found it needless to pursue the lead further."

They walked into the bedroom next to the main entrance. Ketkar stood at the door, while Roy moved in to have a look. "This is the sister's room. Her name is Alina. We have given the room a thorough sweep, but were unable to find anything," Roy thought he caught a hint of disappointment in Ketkar's voice.

Roy was amazed as to how bare the sister's room was. While the other parts of the apartment were a study in luxury, this room in contrast had just a bed, a single door almirah and a corner table with a score of biology books neatly stacked on top of each other. "Anyone in the family apart from him and his sister?" he asked while flipping through the books.

"No. Arun was a bachelor all his life – used to say that he is married to his work. Both his parents had died in the 2004 tsunami. Arun was heartbroken when it happened, but toughened it out for the sake of Alina. She was the only one he could call his own."

More than words, it is the worlds we build that are honest portrayals of our being, Roy thought. And to him, it was the sister's loneliness that manifested around the empty room. "Tell me something more about her," he asked.

"She is twenty-three, a freakily smart girl," Ketkar said. "Top of her class throughout; currently working with

NewTech Ltd as a biophysicist." Should have guessed with all the biology books about, Roy thought.

"She always keeps to herself, has neither friends nor acquaintances and hardly speaks to anyone. Her routine for all seven days consists of a morning jog before going straight to the lab. She spends the rest of the day there and comes home only late at night."

"She must have been pretty close to her brother?" Roy asked.

"Not really. The nineteen-year age difference meant that he was virtually a father figure to her. He was quite protective of Alina, having looked after her since adolescence. But though he always kept an eye on her, they hardly spoke," Ketkar said. "And there is one more thing...but I don't know whether I should be telling you this. If our old friend gets even a hint of it, I will be in a soup..."

Roy instantly knew who Ketkar was referring to. Even though it had now been a year since Roy last saw Shantanu, but like a festering flesh wound, the name still cracked up his skin. "I would be the last one to speak to him."

"Yes, I know," Ketkar said with a sympathetic smile. "And this goes for you too, not a word to the boss," he said pointing his finger at Romil, "You have never met Roy, don't know how he looks like and have not even heard his name. Clear?"

"Yes sir," Romil said with nervous sincerity.

"Actually, Alina is our prime suspect," Ketkar said. He paused for a moment to let Roy digest the information. "We believe we have a strong case against her, and frankly I think it would be difficult for her to get out of this."

"What makes you so sure of it?" his years in the crime branch made Roy suspect everything detectives say.

"Let me show you," Ketkar said. He walked Roy over to the other room in the house. "This is Arun's room; also where his body was found."

The police had a put tape across Arun's room to keep trespassers out. But to Roy, the tape seemed unnecessary, for he had been to many such rooms and in all these places, death seemed to whisper from within; warning people against coming inside.

Ketkar removed the tape and opened the door. The room had a king sized bed, a couple of side tables, a mini refrigerator, a treadmill towards the right and a wardrobe occupying the entirety of the left wall. The room had only one window. The view was that of a wide boulevard, lined with tall Ashok trees on either side.

"The autopsy states that the murder was committed between three and four a.m. on the night of the fourteenth," Ketkar said. "The Powai police station received a call at around 3:45 a.m. from a neighbour, saying he heard a loud bang, like that of a gun going off. The team reached at about 4:00 a.m. No one answered the bell, so they pried open the main gate of the flat. The door of Arun's room was shut, but unlocked. The police went inside to find the body in a sitting position, propped up against the wall, right next to the mini refrigerator over there." Ketkar signalled towards a human figure in a sitting position chalked out on the wall.

"Alina's door was bolted from inside. The police banged on it for a good fifteen minutes before she came out. I think you will find what the commanding officer wrote in his report about her demeanour interesting – she looked disoriented. In all probability, she was either intoxicated or drugged and questioned our presence. On being informed of her brother's demise, she said that she knew nothing of it, and was most surprised and inquired how it had come about. In my opinion, she was calm and placid, more inquisitive than shocked at the news."

Ketkar was speaking and moving swiftly, completely in his elements. Roy knew that it meant Ketkar was certain that he had found his culprit. "I tell you, Konte, they made a big mistake by not taking her blood sample there and then. Her reaction makes me believe we would have found some incriminating substance in her veins," he said.

"What about the autopsy?" Roy asked as he moved towards the chalked outline. "No, no, don't touch anything," Ketkar yelled. Roy moved back. He would have to come in later for a more thorough examination, he thought.

"The autopsy states that the murder was committed using a single barrel 12 gauge shotgun. There was just one bullet wound right in the heart, which had been enough to do the job. The shirt that Arun wore had a two inch hole, where the bullet had passed. The murder weapon, a Beretta 410, was found under the bed – with Alina and Arun's fingerprints all over it. The shotgun was registered in Arun's name who had bought it last year, ironically, for self-protection."

"Self-protection? Did he feel that he was in some kind of danger?" Roy asked.

"Nothing concrete. But his friends say that with the kind of wealth Arun had accumulated in recent years, he felt he ought to be more careful, and supposed a shotgun would be an ideal weapon to keep handy."

"It is with guns, just as it is with people," Roy said, "the most hurt is caused by the ones kept close. Anyone else who might have entered the apartment?"

"No sign of anyone else being in the apartment; no evidence of forced entry either. Thankfully, we have CCTV camera footage which confirms that no strangers came into the building."

"I see what makes you so sure about his sister being the culprit," Roy said. "But to prove your case to courts, you would need to have a motive."

"Arun was a rich man, with no wife or kids and everything now stands to go to Alina. Money is the biggest motivation there is, my friend," Ketkar said. "On top of it, acquaintances have testified that Alina never talked to her brother directly and the neighbours heard them quarrelling often."

"This is starting to look like very much an open and shut case," Roy agreed ruefully. "I am afraid I might not be left with much to do." He walked over to the bullet marks on the wall, and peered at them closely. For some reason they were not making sense to him, but it might just have been his mind that was playing tricks. "Tell me more about his sister," he asked.

"She does not have any friends or hobbies to speak of, but staying fit is an obsession. There is a gym on the terrace of her lab and she religiously spends a couple of hours there at least five days a week. On the night of the murder, she came home at about midnight after a workout. She claims she went straight to her room, freshened up, ate her dinner and went to bed. She usually likes to read for an hour before going to bed, but that day she wasn't feeling well. Thereafter, all she remembers is the police pounding on her door."

"I see. Did the forensics find anything?" Roy asked hesitatingly.

"No. They came in at about nine in the morning, full five hours after the police team had been all over the crime scene.

The fellow in charge said that they couldn't have come earlier as his shift starts only from eight. He took a cursory look, collected a few samples and concluded that there was nothing to be found," Ketkar placed his arm on Roy's shoulder. "The forensics team hasn't been the same since you left."

Roy walked away from Ketkar, towards the window, and stared at the Ashok trees. He couldn't deny he missed his old job, but didn't want to think of the past.

"Anyway, Roy," Ketkar said. "I have told you all that I know."

"Thanks, Ketkar. I owe you one," Roy said as he pressed for the elevator. Ketkar wanted to give Roy a hug, and tell him how proud he was on seeing Roy stand on his feet again, but he just nodded his head in acknowledgement.

"Ketkar sir, who was he?" Romil asked upon the closing of the elevator doors.

"He, my boy, was the only righteous person to have walked into our department," Ketkar said, and mumbled softly, "And has been paying the price ever since." Romil was not sure he understood what Ketkar meant.

Roy called Chandra as soon as he stepped out of the building. "What took you so long?" Chandra asked, "Come over to our office right away. Ask anyone for directions to the Hiranandani Hub. We are on the fifth floor, C Wing. I haven't got all day, make it fast."

The Banker's Lair

The rain had ebbed to a drizzle, and was accompanied by a soothing wet breeze. Though Roy had noticed the urgency in Chandra's voice, he left the bike behind and decided to walk the distance. He had always hated taking orders, and couldn't care less about what Chandra or anyone else thought.

It was 1 p.m. by the time he reached the Fox Capital offices. A young receptionist, dressed sharply in a striped shirt and a black skirt gave Roy a visitors' access card and asked him to follow her. She led him to the upper offices; the clanking of her stilettos reverberating across the corridor. The stilettos stopped outside a frosted door. The cabin had 'Mr Chandra M. Naidu, Executive Assistant to the CEO' engraved on it, with a signboard requesting the visitors to knock before entering. The receptionist went in, signalling Roy to wait outside. She emerged a couple of minutes later. "Mr Naidu will see you now."

"Ah, Mr Konte. You have kept us waiting, take a seat," Chandra said.

Roy ignored the jibe. "Why are you conducting a separate investigation when the police are already looking into it?" he jumped straight to the question that had been nagging him all morning.

Chandra responded calmly. "Mr. Konte, in our line of commerce, we have a fiduciary responsibility towards our clients." Chandra always fell back to his official behaviour when in an unfamiliar situation. "Naturally, it is critical that we not only preserve their trust, but also defend against even the slightest perception of risk. Hence, it is vital that the whole affair does not get any more sordid than it already has. We want to know all the facts and can't trust the police to be forthcoming on the details. We need someone on the inside in order to be in a better position to respond to our clients." Roy was unconvinced, but did not press further. "Given the sensitivity of the matter, we have taken the liberty of running a background check on you," Chandra said. Roy kept a blank face as he watched Chandra take out a file from the top drawer of his desk.

"Mr Konte, we might not have begun on a conciliatory footing, but I believe you will agree with me that your case history leaves a lot to be desired." Chandra said as he flipped a page. "You lost your parents quite early in your childhood and grew up in a foster home. There you did well to keep out of trouble and managed to concentrate on studies. You completed your Bachelors in Forensic Science from Mumbai University, and got into the Forensics team of the Mumbai Crime Branch. All impressive," he smiled at Roy, and gently patted on the file.

"But this is where everything starts to go horribly wrong," he said. "Your superiors started to regularly report you for insubordination and unprofessionalism at the Crime Branch." Roy could have corrected him and said that there was just one senior who reported him multiple times, but he was getting tired of this nonsense and wanted it to end as quickly as possible.

"Roughly two years into the job, a charge of 'tampering with evidence' was levied on you," Chandra said. "This led to you being fired, and since then you have remained out of active employment. It has been only a few months since you opened an investigative agency and the cases you investigated have related to either conducting background checks on prospective spouses or locating lost pets. A move to locating missing pets from a respectable job in the Crime Branch does not look like a great career move to me," he said in a mocking voice.

Chandra closed the file and added dismissively, "In short, I can safely conclude that you are terribly unsuited for this job. Now unless you can say something to change my mind in the next five minutes, I would have to say that our little correspondence is over."

Roy kept looking straight into his eyes, as if staring into the depths of his very soul. When he spoke, his voice was calm, but firm, "Mr Chandra, let me remind you that it was you who got in touch with me and asked me to look into the case. I was only doing you a favour in conducting preliminary inquiries into the murder, all on my own expense and time. I will not deny that I was hoping to make some money by offering you my services, but it now seems that I have been unaware of how you and your firm conducts its affairs," Roy was similarly formal in his firmness.

"And as far as my detective capabilities go," he said, "I have been making a few calls in the twenty minutes it took for me to walk to your office. These twenty minutes have told me that you began as a proprietary trader in the firm – entrusted with investing the firms' money in the stock market. It was quite interesting to learn that you made huge losses by betting a big chunk of the portfolio on a single stock just before that company collapsed; a foolish blunder in your line of work," Roy was not mincing any words now. "You would have been fired along with the rest of the staff, if not for Jayesh taking pity on you and hiring you as his personal assistant. And excuse me for saying so, but from a trader to an assistant sure does not seem like a bright career move to me." Chandra jerked back in his chair, his face contorting into that of someone who had just seen a ghost. He could only stare at Roy, who stood up and gently walked out of the cabin.

Roy felt relieved to be out of the room. But now, walking past those corridors, he could not deny that he had been looking forward to work on the case. Not for money or fame, but for the hunger that burnt inside. It was to bring closure to crimes like these that his adolescence had decided to join the crime branch. And if he was able to solve just one such case, he felt he would not have betrayed his youth.

Roy handed back the visitor's card to the receptionist and turned to leave. But the receptionist was speaking on the phone and signalled him to wait. "Mr Jayesh Kumar wants to see you," she said after hanging up the phone. Given the fate of the last meeting, Roy wanted to decline the request, but his needs got better of his annoyance and he once again found himself following the clanking footsteps.

The receptionist knocked and asked Roy to follow her into an empty office. This office was larger and expansively furnished. A sturdy teak desk surrounded by three leather chairs occupied the centre of the office. On the left, there was an L-shaped lounge sofa and on the floor a miniature golf set was laid out. The right wall had been done completely in white, and at the centre was hung one of Raza's famous bindu paintings. Besides the painting, almost hidden from sight was a smaller door.

This door was answered by a butler who welcomed Roy in to another chamber. Roy walked inside the dark and cosy room furnished with all the amenities of an apartment – a bed, a recliner, a wardrobe, a television and a refrigerator, all neatly arranged inside the room. Roy noticed that there were various bottles of medicines and sleeping pills arranged on the bedside table.

Jayesh sat on a recliner, dressed casually in a cream shirt, linen trousers and hotel slippers, with the air of a man who no longer needed to follow dress codes. His frame was thin, fit and his face had a weathered look about it – of someone who had learnt the ropes the hard way. The wrinkles on his face suggested he was in his early sixties, but his fitness would have put a forty-year-old man to shame. He had a disarming charm about him, which lent an extra bit of enigma to the strange room.

"Hi, I am Jayesh," he said in a hoarse, but calm voice.

Roy felt overpowered on being in the presence of someone of Jayesh's stature. He timidly stepped forward to shake his hands. Oddly, Jayesh had a feeble grip; his hands shook nervously, sweating even in the air conditioned room. Roy assumed that Jayesh was either sick or deeply moved by Arun's death. Jayesh sat on the bed, while Roy took the recliner seat, careful to sit erect. Jayesh took some deep breaths, as if trying to steady himself before speaking, "Arun was like a younger brother to me," his voice had found the composure that his body was searching for. "I want you to catch the culprit, come what may..."

"Mr Kumar..." Roy began...

"Please call me Jayesh."

"Yes, Jayesh," Roy said. "Before we begin, I just want to put it up front that I am still undecided on whether I will take the case..."

Jayesh replied in an assuring I-know-it-all voice, "I am aware of what happened between you and Chandra. My instructions to him were to simply contact you and introduce you to me. I don't know why he was snooping into your personal affairs. Rest assured that he will not be bothering you going forward."

"Chandra has nothing to do with this," Roy said. "He had given away pretty quickly that he does not have much authority. Real power does not speak, only the desire for power does. In our line of business we develop the sense to separate the two," his tone implying that he had placed Jayesh into the former category.

Jayesh felt assured that he had hired the right man for the job. "Then what is the issue?" he asked.

"I am not sure whether I would be able to do justice to this assignment," Roy said, admitting his insecurities to himself rather than to Jayesh. "A murder is not something that I have ever investigated in my individual capacity. On top of that, the police team is all over the place and the crime scene has already been contaminated. I don't know whether I will be able to bring any value to the table."

Jayesh clasped and unclasped his hands, mulling over what Roy had said. "Just give me your word that you are going to try your best and I shall be satisfied. I don't expect you to go there with a magic wand and solve everything; but any lack of commitment would be disappointing. Even if you are not able to solve the case, your tenacity will ensure that the police are on their toes."

"But how am I supposed to have access to the inquiry. I am just a civilian," Roy said.

"Don't worry about that. I can talk to people to ensure that you get all the help you need."

Roy was never in doubt of the clout that the wealth exerts in Mumbai, but even he was surprised that Jayesh was claiming to get him full access to such a well-publicized homicide. "And you do understand that my expenses on the case would be on top of my fees," Roy regretted the moment he uttered this comment.

Jayesh pretended not to mind. "Yes, of course. You stand to be well rewarded. At the end of the meeting I will ask my manager to go over all the money matters with you. Feel free to add anything you want."

Though the offer was good, Roy still felt uncomfortable accepting the assignment. Ketkar had made it clear that it was an open and shut case, and Roy did not see it otherwise. Then what was the point of him being a pair of second eyes for 'money to burn' Jayesh? And, wasn't it illegal for him to have access to evidence? He already had had his fair share of troubles with the police department and didn't want to walk that road again. He decided to throw one last question just to ease his soul. "There are much more capable investigators in Mumbai, why me?"

Jayesh looked perplexed; it was an objection he hadn't anticipated. "I thought since you stay close by, you must be familiar with the neighbourhood and the people staying here."

Jayesh noticed that Roy was unconvinced. He added further, "I have hired you because you have been highly recommended by one of your erstwhile colleagues in the Crime Branch. He is a friend of mine, but I am not at liberty to name him. He told me that you are honest and persevering in your craft. Integrity is very important in our profession. All our dealings are based on trust and it is this parameter to which I gave the highest weightage when approaching you."

It was soothing for Roy to know that he had been chosen for his abilities, and was not a name at the end of the coin toss. He picked up the cup of tea, feeling more at ease to continue with the conversation, "I am sure you know that police are convinced it was Alina?"

"What can I say? I have been presented just the police's side of the story. It seemed convincing enough," Jayesh said, trying not to bring in biases in his statement. "With the limited interaction I have had with her, I found her to be nice and bright. I agree if she is guilty, she should be punished, but I just can't see her murdering her brother."

"How long have you known her?" Roy asked.

"As long as I've known Arun, though I must admit I don't recall speaking to her much at all. Our conversations were limited to the times she came to visit Arun at the office; rare occasions themselves."

"But you must have formed some opinion of her?" Roy asked while sipping tea.

"There are little things not worthy of comment, but her most remarkable aspect is her insane intelligence, like an academic wizard. This I know because Arun used to often ask her for help whenever he was tangled up in something complicated."

"You see," Jayesh added, sensing that some explanation was necessary, "What we do in our company can sometimes involve structuring pretty complex products around the specific needs of our clients. Now Arun was himself a top player in this field, but even for him the intricacies involved could get difficult at times. He used to take those home for Alina to work on. And next day, he would come back with a bunch of excel sheets in his computer with clearly defined structure and water tight clauses. It was quite remarkable for someone not trained in finance. I haven't seen anyone like her who was able to understand these things with such clarity."

Roy noted that Jayesh's account of Alina's abilities corroborated with what Ketkar had told him of her. "Have you met her since the incident?" he asked Jayesh.

"On the night of the murder itself," Jayesh said. "Apart from the police, I was the first one to reach there. Someone from the police station had called me. They knew me, and knew that Arun worked with me."

"And, how would you describe her demeanour that night? The police team mentioned that she was calm and placid."

"I agree that there was no hysteria – none of the wailing and crying. It might have come as a surprise for someone who didn't know her. I dare say even an indication of guilt. But I personally thought that she was in a state of shock, and it was easy to see why. Apart from the grief of Arun's death, she was forced to deal with the police's line of enquiry. I asked them to reserve their questioning for later and took Alina to her room. She sat there motionless, not uttering a word. There was no way she could have spent the night in that apartment, so I packed up her bags and checked her into the Renaissance Hotel. I asked the hotel manager to keep an eye on her and to inform me in case anything cropped up. That was the last I heard from her."

Jayesh took off his slippers and stretched his legs on the bed. Roy wondered whether Jayesh wanted him to take leave, but then he spoke, "At my stage of life, one is careful to not add to one's sins. I will not tell you to go easy on Alina, but if Arun's sister is innocent and still gets convicted, I will not be able to forgive myself. It is bad enough that I could not save Arun, but I intend to help his sister in every way I can. I urge you to pursue all lines of enquiries within the realms of possibility. Even if there is a miniscule doubt, I want it thoroughly checked."

"Sure, Jayesh. I'll do my best," Roy finished his cup with a final long slurp and took his leave. As instructed by Jayesh, he went straight to the accountant. The accountant explained the terms of the contract, but Roy was still thinking of Jayesh. There was something about him which had pulled Roy towards him. And even though Jayesh was shaken up with grief throughout the meeting, yet Roy felt conscious of having put himself within the influence of a power that could not be ignored.

Man in the Yellow Shirt

Roy walked out of Fox Capital a lighter man. He rang up Ketkar, "I'm taking up the case."

"Good to know," Ketkar said.

To Roy, it seemed Ketkar was less pleased on hearing the news than he had anticipated, but maybe it was the toll of the work that was getting to him. "There is one thing I would need your help on," Roy said. "I wanted to take a look at the forensic report and other details of the case."

Ketkar responded after a brief pause. "Roy, I do want to help you, but there is no way I will be able to give you access to those files without Shantanu's permission."

"I see," Ketkar could hear the disappointment in Roy's voice.

"Look Konte, I know all about the history between you and Shantanu, but this is something that I just won't be able to do without his approval."

"I understand your position. Thanks anyway," Roy said, disconnecting the call.

Roy went back to his apartment and pondered on his next step. He would have to give Jayesh time to get him access to the police files. But it would be foolish to wait and let the case slip from his grasp. He decided to call Alina. The lobby receptionist picked up the call.

"I want to be connected to 905," he said. Jayesh had already told Roy that Alina was staying in that room.

"Wait a minute." There was a pause at the other end. "I am sorry sir, but the occupant of room 905 has asked us to hold all calls."

Roy could have called Jayesh to get Alina's mobile, but he did not want to bother him unnecessarily. He decided to take a gamble. "I am calling from the police department and this is in reference to a murder that we are investigating. If you don't patch me through to her, then we might have to come down to the hotel. I personally would not like to inconvenience your guests, but you would have left me with no option."

"Let me check with the manager," she said nervously. "Thank you for being patient with us sir," the receptionist was a lot more courteous. "Perhaps we can make an exception this time. Please hold on while we connect you to the room."

Alina lay on her bed, looking up at the ceiling when the telephone rang. She had been clear that she did not want to receive any calls. Had he managed to find her here too? Anxiously, she picked up the receiver. "Hello," she said.

Roy sensed an air of nervousness in her voice, but he put it down to the pressures of the case. "Hi Alina, this is Roy. I am conducting an investigation into Arun's death. I am aware that this is not the best time, but it is very important that I speak to you."

Alina assumed that it was a call from the police department. "What do you want? I have told you guys everything that you wanted to know. I don't have anything to add," she shouted angrily, yet relieved that it was not the one she feared.

"I am not from the police. Jayesh has hired me in his personal capacity," Roy clarified.

Jayesh's name seemed to have softened her a bit. "I see. I am grateful to him for all his help, but I want to be left in peace. Leave your number with the hotel reception. I will call you if I have anything to say." She disconnected without waiting for a reply.

The disturbance out of way, Alina lay back again, pondering over how her life had shaped in the past few days. Arun's death was just as tragic as the death of her parents. But this time, she was left utterly alone. The only way she could cope with the loss was to keep herself busy and resolved to get immersed in the laboratory. She was on the verge of a breakthrough development in paddy crop – which would make them resistant to pesticide poisoning. This was something that could fill up most of her time, she reasoned. Second thing that she had to deal with was the police. Their aggressive line of questioning seemed to hint that she was a suspect. Perhaps she may ask this detective hired by Jayesh for help.

But her immediate problem was the threatening calls she had been receiving since morning. At first she thought him to be a heartbroken lover, but the persistent calls and subsequent death threats convinced her that this was something far more serious. She had switched off her mobile and asked the receptionist to put all calls on hold. But she was concerned that a lot of people knew she was staying at the Renaissance. And if this detective was able to get through to her room, how difficult could it be for the stalker to find her as well.

She felt scared and in that moment of helplessness, she saw herself being carried over to her mother's lap sleeping outside under the winter sun. But Alina's memories were broken by the shrill ring of the room phone, and this time, it was not Roy on the other side of the line.

▼

Roy hung up the phone, took a shower and lit a cigarette. He was trying to keep his smoking to a minimum, lighting up only when he needed to think. The call with Alina had been a failure. The only way to move ahead with the investigation now would be to go meet Shantanu and request him for help with the case files. Their last meeting had been a year back, ending with Roy swearing never to see Shantanu again. Meeting him to ask for help meant Roy would not only need to swallow his pride, but also face a Shantanu determined to make the most of the opportunity. Roy was not sure whether this was something he was ready for, but it was something that there was no escaping from.

An hour later, he found himself in the visitor's chair of the cabin, with his back to the door. Everything in the cabin was just as Roy had left it – the peach coloured curtains, steel cabinets lined across the left and the out-dated calendar hiding the discoloured patch on the wall – all reminding him of a moment frozen still in time. The centre of the room was occupied by a huge oak desk with a wooden plaque that read 'Shantanu Das, Deputy Commissioner of Police'. The secretary had informed Roy that Shantanu was out running an errand and would be back soon. He had been waiting for an agonizing fifteen minutes, when the conversations in the outside corridor came to a sudden halt and everyone hurried back to the desks like rats scurrying off to their holes. This was the sure signal to the arrival of his host.

The cabin door swivelled open. A short lanky man with an erect frame and well-oiled side parted hair walked in with an authoritative air. He was comfortably beyond the middle years of life with a face marked with discipline, but which even in his younger days could not have exuded any love or warmth. He wore a neatly pressed, but faded blue shirt, black thick rimmed glasses and tight fitting pleated trousers – everything exuded the discipline and the staleness of a bygone era. The figure walked right past Roy and took the opposite chair, completely ignoring the earlier occupant of the cabin. He took out a file from his cabinet and started to flip the pages, glancing but not really looking at the contents.

"Hello, Shantanu," Roy finally mustered.

"Oh hello Mr Konte, what a pleasure it is to see you," Shantanu said. "I noticed you when I walked in, but since I remember you saying that you would not want to speak to me again, I thought it would be impolite of me to try and strike up a conversation. Tell me, how can this humble servant be of any use to you?" he flashed a beaming smile at Roy.

Roy wanted to get up and walk away, but a sense of duty kept him glued to the chair. "Shantanu, I have been hired by my client to look into Mr Arun Ruia's murder."

"So I have heard. I must say that the guys at Fox Capital are discerning in recognising your capabilities, while others may have just looked at your failures."

He was not going to make it easy. "As I was saying, for the purpose of my investigation, I would want to have a look at the police files," Roy said.

"I know, I know. Your wish is the department's command," he said as he leaned back on his chair. "You have some influential friends. I have received orders from the head office to make all the files available to you. So I will not be doing you any favour when I say that you have my permission to go over them."

Roy was pleased that Jayesh had been true to his word. "Then thank you; that would be all." Roy got up to walk out.

"Wait, Mr Konte. Sit down. Let me offer you some tea or a cola."

"No, my work is done. I will leave now." Roy did not care if he sounded rude.

"You have remained the same Mr Konte, always a problem with authority." Shantanu closed his file, placed his palms on his desk and propped forward towards Roy. "I don't like anyone interfering with my investigations, least of all you. In this case, however, my hands are tied. But before you begin nosing around in our affairs, let me make one thing clear to you. Even though you might have made some powerful friends, I assure you they will not be able to save you if you do anything to hamper this investigation. And that goes for your friend Ketkar as well. I have called him to let you have access to the files, but do warn him on my behalf that his neck will also be on the line in case you bungle up."

"If that would be all..." Roy replied curtly and proceeded towards the door.

Shantanu shot from behind, "I want you to know that I don't have anything personal against you. I have always been just trying to do my job as honestly as possible, and I will not hesitate to do the right thing this time too." Roy walked out without a reply.

▼

The figure stood on the footpath right across Hotel Renaissance. He chose this particular spot, as it offered his binoculars a clear view of room 905. He was carrying a small umbrella which was only partly able to shelter him from the rain. His yellow shirt had mending patches all over the sides, and the seams of his trousers had come off due to regular use. It was but natural that he looked pensive, for his brother had been missing for the past four days. At first, he did not think much of the disappearance, as it was usual for his brother to not come home for days together.

But his suspicions took firmer shape when he read about Arun's death in the papers. He had a friend working as a constable in the Powai police station, and it is from him that he got Alina's phone number and her present location. He had been calling her on her mobile since morning, hoping to threaten her into revealing something about his brother's disappearance, but she kept disconnecting his calls. He dialled in to the hotel. Though it took quite long to convince the receptionist that he was Alina's lab assistant calling about an urgent business, the receptionist eventually let him through. He could tell from Alina's voice that this time she was completely rattled. He smiled from the small pleasure it gave him. She must have finally realised that he was going to pursue her till the end of the world.

After getting rid of Shantanu, Roy went straight to meet Ketkar at his Bandra station. Ketkar preferred to spend his time at this station rather than the headquarters so that he could be as far from Shantanu as possible. There was another reason why Ketkar liked this station. It was located right between a sweet shop and a bar – and Ketkar was a regular customer for both. Roy found Ketkar sitting in his office, munching on samosa paavs, with a table fan right against his face to cool him down.

"Here comes the hero," Ketkar was never short of a kind word to Roy. "Pray have a seat. I heard you managed to snatch the meat from the jaws of the shark himself. You should have heard Shantanu's voice when he told me to allow you to have the case files. I confirmed twice just to irk the bugger." Ketkar was throwing out pieces of his snack as he struggled to control his chortle.

"Nothing that I did," Roy said. He was still struggling to fathom how Jayesh had managed to pull this one off.

"Doesn't matter. Shantanu can't do a thing to stop it now. I have sent all the files to be photocopied to save you the trouble of coming for them repeatedly." Then he turned serious. "But make sure not to leak anything of what is in the report to anyone; especially Alina."

"Yes, I know," Roy assured Ketkar.

"Well, if that is all done and settled," Ketkar said, his eyebrows twitching with excitement. "Why don't we head down the bar for old time's sake?"

"To the bar, Ketkar? While on duty?"

Ketkar put down the half-eaten paav on the plate, wiping his mouth with a tissue. "Obviously, I mean, of course...I meant only when I am done. I obviously don't drink while on duty."

Roy kept staring at him reproachfully, but could not control himself any longer and burst into a laugh. Ketkar also relaxed and joined in with a smile.

"You bugger. This is not the way to treat an old friend." He picked up his snack again. "What say? Tonight at my place. I have saved up a nice bottle of scotch – seal still intact."

"Why not, sir? We have a lot to catch up..." He was interrupted by his phone ringing. "Yes, this is Roy here..."

Ketkar saw Roy getting serious, mumbling only in monosyllables.

"No worries. I will be there right away," he said as he disconnected the call. "Sorry Ketkar, I will have to leave. Something urgent came up. Please keep those files handy, I will pick them up later."

"What happened all of a sudden?" Ketkar asked.

"Nothing, sir, a silly errand that I have to take care of," Roy shot back while hurrying out of the cabin. Ketkar could always sense when he was being lied to. He knew Roy was hiding something from him, but he let his old friend be.

The man in the yellow shirt had spent forty-five minutes on the road, when he saw a pair of eyes through the windows of room 905. Alina stared at him and his binoculars for a couple of seconds before quickly swaying away. The man was unsure of what to do next. It was clear that she had figured out that it was he who was after her; perhaps she would try to get out of the hotel. He quickly ran towards the front entrance of the hotel and made it just in time to catch a glimpse of her slipping into a hotel car. He ran towards the nearest cab and asked the driver to follow the car.

Alina's car took a left turn, then another left turn into the Link Road and then a right, on course towards the Hiranandani all the while with the cab in pursuit. Then five minutes into the chase, Alina's car suddenly accelerated, swerving to get past the cars in front. She has figured out that she is being followed, he thought. He slipped in a hundred rupee note to the cab driver, asking him to ensure that the car did not get away; he checked his pockets to make sure he had enough left for the fare.

Alina's car took a series of twists and turns, accelerating and breaking at short intervals, but her tail kept up the chase. After playing this game for a good fifteen minutes, her car came to a sudden halt outside the Hiranandani dispensary. She calmly got out of the car and walked into the dispensary. He was puzzled at her sudden stop. Could it be that she hadn't grasped that she was being followed. Was he imagining things when he saw her trying to get rid of the cab? He waited for a few minutes thinking what he could do. Then getting impatient, he decided to walk into the dispensary and confront her there itself.

With resolute steps, he got out of the cab and walked into the shop. It was teeming with customers, but he could not spot Alina among them. Panicking, he went to the counter and asked the cashier about the lady who had just entered the dispensary, giving him Alina's description.

"Oh, I see. You must be talking about Alina madam. She is one of our regular customers. You are right; she came in a few minutes before and asked me if she could use the restroom. But I haven't seen her since. She might have gone out through the door next to the restroom."

The First Meeting

Alina's car came to a halt at the three-storied dilapidated structure that she had been directed to. The building walls had been left unpainted, the window frames were hanging by the hinges and half a dozen idlers were hunched over a card game by the side of the gates. She double checked the address from the piece of paper she had been holding. She had hurriedly taken down the instructions while on the chase; but looking up at the building, she would not have been disappointed if it turned out to be the incorrect address.

The door was answered by a tall, lanky man dressed in an untucked shirt and loosely hanging trousers. His hair carelessly fell on his forehead, while his lips were burnt from tobacco smoke. Though his face had been moulded into the maturity of a middle-aged man, she was sure he wasn't a day above twenty-five. "Hi, please come in," Roy said as he welcomed his unlikely guest.

The living room was barely furnished with a couple of chairs lined against the left walls and a mattress thrown in the centre. Newspapers were all stacked beside the bedroom gate, while a couple of bed sheets had been used to prevent the sunlight from filtering in. It seemed that Roy had spent the last few minutes making the apartment look presentable, but had failed miserably. Alina went in and sat in one of the corner chairs.

She said, "I am sorry to bother you so suddenly. I had tried Jayesh's mobile, but he was not picking up. I don't know anyone else whom I could call. Since you have been selected by Jayesh, I thought..."

"Yes...yes, you did the right thing," Roy assured her.

"Do you think I should go to the police with this?" she asked.

Roy knew the direction in which the police investigation was heading. At this point he was not sure whether this incident would be beneficial or detrimental to her case. "This is a sensitive matter and I would request you to keep it contained to as few people as possible," he said. "It is best if you first give me the details of everything that has happened and then we can decide how to go about it." It occurred to him that he had not offered her anything yet. "Would you like some tea or coffee?"

"Yes, a cup of coffee would be nice," she said.

Alina sat in a corner which Roy could see from the kitchen window. She had straight black hair, pouty lips and small eyes, all set in a beautiful face; a study in contrast to his shabbily furnished apartment. She was elegantly dressed in a black top and knee length skirt and he could see the hours spent in the gym in her toned arms and sculpted legs. She had a personality that commanded attention, and a demeanour comfortable with it. But the thing that impressed him most was the way in which Alina held her composure. She had lost her brother, had been incessantly questioned by the police and chased by an unknown man soon after; but there she sat, in a complete stranger's house, patiently waiting for her coffee.

"Here you go," Roy said as he handed her a cup. "Now, tell me what happened."

"Well, there is nothing much to be told," Alina said jerking her head to remove the strands of her hair which had fallen on to her face. "He had been calling me since the morning, first on my mobile and then at the hotel." That is why her voice had been so tense when I called, Roy thought, secretly feeling happy that the frostiness did not have anything to do with something he might have done. "Then this evening I found him looking up at my room, and I have already told you the story after."

"Anyone in particular you suspect? Any enemies or perhaps an old ex-boyfriend?" Roy asked sheepishly.

"No, cannot think of anyone. There is hardly anyone I meet."

"We cannot dismiss the possibility that it may have a connection with what happened with your brother. And if that is the case, then it will not do to simply shake the stalker off. We will have to try and find out who he is, and what he is looking for." He paused, waiting for Alina to say something, but she kept quiet.

"Let us go over what information we have on him. How many times did he call you since the morning?"

"About six times on my mobile and twice at the hotel," Alina replied.

"And did he keep calling you from the same number?"

"Yes, I have it in my call records."

"This is not smart of him to not switch numbers…sounds like a novice. Anyways, we are not the ones who should be complaining; it gives us a strong starting point to work with. Did you get a good look at him when you were being chased?"

"No, not even a glance. I did see him when he was standing outside the hotel, but he was too far down for me to make out his features."

Roy kept silent for the next few minutes, his chin resting on his palm. "You said that you got rid of him by walking in and out of the dispensary, taking the alternate exit." Alina nodded. "Then it very well might be that he went into the dispensary looking for you and even asked around for you. It's likely that the dispensary would have a security camera. That way, we would be able to get a visual on him."

"Sounds promising," Alina said.

"But it's not safe to go to the shop this evening. He might still be hanging around. We will have to save that for tomorrow. For now, give me the number that he had been calling you from. I know just the person who could help us with it."

Roy dialled a number on his phone and spoke for a few minutes. "That was Asif, an old associate of mine. He is a bit of a nut case, but gets the job done. He says he will have a positive ID on the number by tomorrow."

Alina nodded. The few moments spent with her were enough to let Roy know why she was taken to be so reticent. It was difficult to get her talking. And when she did speak, she did so with balance – weighing every word and not uttering two where one would suffice. But right now, he had a more immediate problem that needed to be dealt with. It was late evening and she needed to be safely whisked away to the hotel.

Roy was unsure how comfortable she would be to ride on a bike with a complete stranger, so he opted to drop her in a cab instead. They took the back door to the hotel, lest the stalker may have returned looking for her. For added precaution, he asked the receptionist to check her into a different room, this one looking away from the street. They also did not want to book the room under Alina's name, so he fished out his driving licence and asked the hotel to book the room under his name.

"This was not such a bad day as it might have turned out to be," Alina said. "Thank you for all your help."

"No need to thank me. Just doing the job I am getting paid for," Roy said with a slight bow.

After dropping Alina, Roy returned to his apartment to find Romil waiting for him outside his door.

"Ketkar sir asked me drop these documents for you," Romil said holding out a brown packet.

"It's nice of you to have come to deliver these past your working hours. Why don't you come inside for a drink?"

"I don't drink sir," Romil said defensively. "I hope you don't mind."

Shantanu must have kept him on a tight leash; Roy felt sorry for the boy. "Not at all Romil," he said. "Thanks again for the documents and have a nice evening."

Roy went inside the apartment, laid the case files on the chair and threw himself on the bed. It had been a long day, and the next few days weren't going to be easy either.

Alina had set up her alarm for seven, but woke up at six. Sleep had been playing hard to get these days. She took a cold shower and went down to the hotel gym. She would have preferred a jog in the lawns, but was not sure whether it was a safe thing to do. Running up the treadmill was the only relaxation she got; the thirty minutes when she thought of nothing but her feet chafing against the rubber.

She went back to the room and checked her mobile. There was a missed call. For a second she was nervous, but was relieved when she saw Jayesh's name on the screen. She dialled him back. "Hello Jayesh uncle, you called?"

"Yes child." She noticed that he had taken to calling her that ever since Arun died. "Just checking up on you. Everything all right there?."

"Yes, everything is fine uncle." She didn't want to bother him unnecessarily with all the details.

"Nice to know, be sure to call me in case you need anything. Please don't hesitate," he said.

"Sure uncle, I will keep that in mind."

"And one more thing. Did you manage to speak to Roy? I have hired him to help us with the case."

"Yes, we did meet. Nothing much discussed though. He is still collecting information about the case, I think," Alina said.

"I see." Jayesh added after some thought. "Please make sure that you tell him everything about the case. Will do us all some good."

"I will do that," she said.

Alina was grateful for Jayesh's help, and considered it nice of him to ensure her wellbeing. Moreover, most of her money was in Arun's account, and it would take some time for her to withdraw any funds. It was Jayesh who had been providing for all her needs in the interim.

Roy was awoken by his mobile ringing. He looked at the watch. It was 7 a.m. He had no respect for people who disturbed others this early in the morning.

"Asif here," the caller said. "Can I come over?" he asked.

"Sure, what time?" Roy knew Asif never gave any information on the phone.

"I will be there in an hour," Asif said. Roy confirmed the appointment and went back to sleep. His doorbell rang sharp at eight. In walked a man, stoutly built, with a cane in his right hand and a purple cap in his left. His face was scarred and palms roughed, a fellow no one would hire as a salesman. Asif glanced backwards, first towards the left and then to the right.

"Just checking that I am not being followed," he said with a serious air. "I have just discovered that I am on the hit list of both the Chinese and the Pakistani governments. There is nothing called too much precaution." This time he is really outdoing himself, Roy thought and let his guest in. He noticed that Asif's overalls were stinking of alcohol. "What will you have to drink"?

"At eight in the morning? Are you crazy?" Asif placed his stick in the corner. "Well, get me a glass of whiskey, if you must."

Roy fetched a bottle of Royal Stag from the kitchen and poured some into his glass. "Water"?

"You think I am going to have that filthy water? I carry my own bottle. Distilled and pure from their germs," he said with a grunt. He took a small plastic bottle from his pocket and poured it into his drink. "I am telling you this because I like you." He lowered his voice and bent forward. "The Chinese have been polluting our water. I have solid information that they have mixed a concoction of seeds and manure in the city water supply. Give it a year, we all will be growing weeds out of our intestines."

Bizarre as they sounded, Asif had firm faith in his theories and did not take kindly to them being questioned. Roy tolerated them for the immense help Asif had been through the years. So he sat patiently as Asif explained the Chinese plot in minute details. The previous time it was the US trying to buyout Mumbai, and before that he was convinced that UK had been helping aliens to carry out an invasion. It was surprising that this same Asif had built a top notch network of informers in and around Mumbai, recruiting everyone from beggars to the milkmen to the courier boys, making it impossible for anything or anyone to fly below his radar. Roy waited for Asif to finish his story.

"So did you find out anything about the number?" Roy asked.

"Ah, I had almost forgotten about that," Asif said, disappointed that Roy did not have any questions on the Chinese plot. He took out a folded piece of paper and held it in front of his face. "Name is Babu Manke Kadam and stays in a chawl at Lower Parel. A small time clerk in a government office. No criminal records, no history of violence."

Roy pulled out a grainy picture from his pocket. "This is the photo I got from the CCTV camera of a dispensary. Is it the same guy?"

Asif put on his glasses and looked at the picture carefully, "Yes, this is the one."

"This is impressive. Thanks for your help." Roy was always amazed by how quickly Asif scooped out the necessary information. He took the paper and slipped it in between the pages of his journal. "What do I owe you, Asif Bhai?"

"Was too easy a job. I will accept this drink to be full payment of my services!" Asif said, holding aloft the empty whiskey glass. "As it is, you will need to save every penny for medical services if you don't stop drinking that filthy water."

Roy called Alina right after Asif's departure. "Hi Alina, got some news for you. Do you know someone by the name of Babu Manke Kadam?"

"No, never heard of the name," she said.

"Strange. He is the person who has been stalking you. Right now, I don't know much about him save his name and address. Will go down there later today to find out more."

Alina thought for a moment. "I also want to be there with you. Want to see for myself who he is. Maybe I will recall something if I see him in person."

Roy considered the proposition. It might be dangerous for her to be there. But then again, there was no denying that Alina had a decent chance of recognizing the stalker if she saw him with her own eyes. "Okay, I will pick you up from the Renaissance in the evening."

Right after hanging up Alina's call, Roy drove towards Fox Capital to give Jayesh his regular update. Within twenty minutes, he was inside the cabin.

"Why do you want yourself to get involved in these things?" Jayesh asked irritably when he heard that Roy was going to confront the stalker. "This does not concern what I have asked you to do. Why don't you ask the police to deal with this problem?"

"I appreciate your concern Jayesh," Roy said, partly miffed with Jayesh's interference. "But the timing of this whole thing makes it likely that it concerns Arun's murder. I want to interrogate him before the police gets on to him. It will be difficult to get hold of him once he is in their custody."

Jayesh stroked his chin. "If you are adamant, I will not stop you. But I have something which might be of some help." He opened his cabinet and fished out a small rusted key hidden below the stationery. He then went to the recliner and removed the right hand rest to reveal a locked compartment built into the chair. He opened the compartment and fetched out a Colt single action pistol. "Take this with you when you go."

Roy was taken aback by the sudden appearance of the pistol. He hadn't expected a man like Jayesh to have a pistol snucked around in office. But it made sense for Roy to take up the offer. After all, he would be fending off for Alina as well. He took out a handkerchief from his pocket, wrapped the pistol in it and thrust it towards the back, inside his trousers.

"One thing I want you to understand Roy," Jayesh said, as Roy was about to leave. "Keep the pistol responsibly, for if you happen to do something funny with that gun, then I am going to deny any recollection of having lent it to you. It is nothing personal to do with you, but I have learnt in life to always keep layers of protection between the problems and myself."

Babu Manke Kadam

Alina could not get the name Babu Manke Kadam out of her mind. It seemed vaguely familiar, but she was unable to lay a finger to it. She shut her eyes, forcing herself to concentrate harder, until it finally hit her. Alina called up the reception and asked them to get her a cab for Hiranandani.

Roy walked out of Jayesh's cabin and headed home. On his way out, he saw Chandra's cabin door open and the light on. He wanted to slip by the cabin quietly, but heard his name called out as soon as he walked across. "Roy," Chandra yelled, running towards the door. "Would you mind stepping in for a couple of minutes?" he said peering out of his cabin.

"I am sorry we had a bad beginning." Chandra said, offering Roy a cup of coffee.

"It's alright. Never a good thing to carry bad blood forward," Roy said, pouring two teaspoons of sugar in his cup. "But I am curious about one thing. Why did you run a check on me? I don't see how that was helping you out."

"I understand you getting miffed about that. But please understand that it was nothing personal," Chandra said. "Jayesh had asked me to do a detailed check on you, and I was trying to make a decent job of it." This was a surprise for Roy, for it contradicted the version Jayesh had laid in front of him. But he considered it best not to probe further.

"If you don't mind, can I ask you a few questions about Arun?" Roy said, making an effort to sound casual.

"Sure, please do. I will help all I can." The change in Chandra's tone within a span of twenty-four hours was remarkable. "What do you want to ask me?"

"Nothing concrete," Roy said, flushing out his pocketbook and a pencil. "Can you give me a sense of what Arun was like to his colleagues? Any friction there?"

Chandra arched back in his chair, his fingers dancing around the paper weight. "Well, I don't want to plant any ideas in your head, but it was no secret that he wasn't the most popular guy around. Sure, he had high expectations and was a stickler for discipline, but these are not the traits we quite mind in our line of work. If you ask me, his unpopularity was due to the layoffs he oversaw during the depression that really put people off," he dropped the paperweight from his fingers and looked into Roy's eyes. "But I think it was a bit unfair on their part to put the firings wholly on him."

"What makes you say that?"

Chandra lowered his voice, as if he was being more frank with Roy than needed. "It was all subtle politics," he said. "You see, Jayesh and Arun pulled up a classic good cop, bad cop routine on the staff. So, while it was Jayesh's plan to cull the staff all along, the whole thing was setup to look like Jayesh was on their side, fighting to keep the casualties to a minimum. This way he was able to keep the morale of the remaining staff high, like a good old grandfather distributing toffees. Of course, the flip side was that Arun came to be hated by the rest, but there is one in every office: the successful guy who has his lunch alone quietly in a corner."

All this was information to Roy; pieces of puzzle that he hoped to eventually fit in to the whole picture. But he was careful to not convey any sense of surprise, for he knew that nothing shuts up a good source than him knowing he is important to the listener. He quietly put his notebook aside, leaving his mind to do all the recording.

"But don't take this to mean that Arun was an innocent fellow. He has wrecked many a career to straighten his path," Chandra added.

"I don't get it," Roy said.

"Do you think I ever wanted to be an assistant?" he let out a sigh. "I had been in this firm since the beginning, much before Arun, and toiled hard to get Fox to where it is now. My trades were making money for the firm and Jayesh consulted me about every decision he made. And then, he came along," Chandra had disgust in his voice. "I could see in his eyes that Arun was eyeing my position, but I was so close to Jayesh that he could not have done anything to dislodge me from my perch. You recall that in our first meeting you had mentioned that terrible trade which landed me in here?"

Of course Roy remembered. It had not been such a difficult thing to find out. The business papers of the time had snippets of the story that Chandra, in spite of being an experienced trader, had gambled a big chunk of the firm's money on the shares of a ship building company, Seafarers Limited. And when that company went bust, so did the investment.

"It had been just five months since Arun joined the firm," Chandra said. "One day, he came up to me and told me that he knew the CEO of Seafarers and the news was that the company was being purchased by a larger shipping company at a huge premium to the prevailing share price. He lured me by saying that the share price was going to quadruple in a month. But I was not one to take everything at face value. I was a seasoned trader and often came across these tips, which more generally than not were simply hot air in a balloon. I was not going to gamble the firm's money based on what a five-month-old employee had to say. Plus, it is illegal to trade based on inside information, and I was wary of any backlash." He then abruptly stopped, as if recognizing the danger he was putting himself in by revealing this information to Roy.

"Please go on," Roy said, sensing Chandra's hesitation. "I am not going to judge you based on your past actions. I am here to solve this case, and anything you say would be used only in context of this case."

"So to convince me, Arun managed to pull off something unthinkable," Chandra continued, more relaxed after Roy's assurance. "He got the CEO of the company to fly down to Mumbai and set up a meeting with me. The CEO of the company was sitting right across this table, in the same chair that you are occupying now. He confirmed that the news was true and for extra effect added that he wouldn't have met me, but because Arun was a dear friend, he was doing this as a favour to him. This was all the confirmation I needed to get my itch going. I sold off half of the firm's investments and put all of it in this single company. Barely two weeks after, Seafarers in a press release stated that the company was filling for bankruptcy. I had to sell off those shares at a huge discount to my purchase price. Needless to say, Jayesh was furious and wanted to fire me right away. But Arun stepped in and suggested that he take me as an assistant instead."

"I see," Roy said. "Did you confront Arun after that?"

"I did, obviously," Chandra said, getting angrier. "But while I was hysterical, he was calm throughout the argument. He said I should thank him for saving my job; it was now in my best interest to keep quiet and not spoil the working relationship by making a big issue out of this thing. He knew that there was nothing much I could do about it. I had placed a trade that was both stupid and illegal. My spilling the beans would have made matters worse for me rather than him." Chandra took a moment to compose himself. "I would be lying to you if I told you that I was terribly disappointed to see him go."

Chandra was aware that he was implicating himself as a possible suspect in Arun's murder. But his urge to let someone know that he had been wronged and that fate itself had intervened to take his revenge had been enough to cloud his good sense.

Alina took the elevator to the seventeenth floor. This was the first time she had been to the flat since Arun's death. Alina fished for the keys inside her purse, almost sorry to have found them straight away. She opened the apartment and paused at the entrance. Standing there outside the door, Alina wondered whether she was asking a lot of herself to assume she would steel her way through. She kept reminding herself that she was doing this for Arun.

Alina went into the flat and headed straight for Arun's room. She realised that the place was still under police investigation and there would be trouble if they realised that she was fiddling through Arun's stuff. Sure they were going to have footage of the CCTV at the entrance, but she could always make an excuse of going in there to get some urgent papers. Entering Arun's room would be much too difficult to explain.

Alina was aware that the police had confiscated Arun's laptop, so she had to try and locate the physical printouts of his bank statements. Those would be somewhere among the documents that he kept in his side table. She opened the drawer and fetched out a bundle of papers. It had the salary slips, the credit card statements, and official documentation of business deals. Finally she located the folder with his bank statements.

She started with the latest monthly statement, August 2015 – nothing in there. On to July, and yes, surely enough, the topmost entry was a Rs. 20,000 debit to the name of Shankar Manke Kadam. She took a picture of the statement on her cell phone. June2015 – another 20,000 debit in Shankar Manke Kadam's name. Same was in case of May, April, March and going back right up to January'2013. Arun did not have copies of the statement prior to that date. She dialled up Roy's number, but he disconnected her call. Alina left a message on his cell phone asking him to get back to her as soon as possible.

Roy saw Alina's call. He was in middle of his interview with Chandra. He could not afford to let anything disturb the conversation – he doubted whether Chandra would be in so frank a mood again. "And can you tell me what kind of relationship was between Jayesh and Arun? Any quarrels or anything that you recall?"

"No, nothing at all," Chandra said. "They were on the most fantastic terms possible. Sure there were some minor disagreements regarding office work, but those were always related to official matters and nothing more. I personally felt, and this is my personal view strictly, that Jayesh was searching for someone like family in Arun. In spite of all his success and money, Jayesh lives alone, with no one of his own to speak of. I got the feeling that Arun was a long lost son to him. Jayesh was always forgiving and kind to him. I don't recall a single incident when Arun asked for something, to which Jayesh did not agree. This was very surprising for a man like Jayesh, who does not give his employees even an inch more than necessary." Chandra thought for a while, as if to say something to substantiate his point. "I will tell you about an incident the other day," he said. "We were working on an important deal we had landed for a bond issue, the kind which come through not more than twice a year. So, we are all together, putting our heads into the presentation with Jayesh preparing to present it to the CEO of the company. The police came in to tell us that Arun's post mortem had been done and the family could claim the body for the last rites. Now granted that the employees had their differences with Arun, still some of us did want to attend his cremation. But Jayesh was having none of it. He made sure that all of us worked on the presentation, while he was the only one who went for the cremation to sort of represent the office."

Though the interview was fruitful, Roy came out of the cabin with more questions than answers. Jayesh's portrait in Chandra's words was very different from the picture that Roy had painted in his mind. He spoke of him as a cunning disciplinarian, while Jayesh had given him the impression of being a caring employer. Roy was not sure whether he understood either Jayesh or Chandra well, or Alina for that matter. It was difficult for him to get rid of the feeling that someone somewhere was playing him as a pawn in this sordid affair.

Romil was going through the police case files for the umpteenth time. It was just like student days for him, where the files were his syllabus and he wanted to make sure that he did not miss out on any chapters. He went through the post mortem report, the testimony of all the employees, the description of the footage from the CCTV camera, Alina's questioning, and interviews with the neighbours and the reports filled by the local police station. This is when he noticed a small discrepancy, not directly related to the case, but something he hoped would give him some brownie points with Ketkar.

He straightaway walked into Ketkar's office, who was lying in a stupor, his back arched in the chair and a piece of cloth covering his face. "Ketkar sir, there is something that I want to tell you," Romil said.

"What is it?" Ketkar said, his irritation apparent in his voice.

"Sir, the photocopies of the files that we sent to Roy…"

Ketkar removed the cloth from his face, interrupting Romil in between, "You haven't told anyone about them, have you?"

"No, nothing of that sort, sir," Romil said. "Just that I had counted all the pages that we handed over to Roy to make sure that I don't misplace any. And today, when I counted the pages that we have in our bundle, I realised that there are two extra sheets. It seems like somehow we missed sending over a couple of pages."

"I see, might have got mixed up while photocopying," Ketkar said. "Good job you noticed. Might be something important. Give me that bundle. I will get in touch with Roy and will make sure to send him the missing pages." Romil walked out of the office, visibly pleased with himself.

Ketkar waited for the office door to close. He then picked up his mobile and dialled a number. "Hello, Ketkar here," he said. "Are you sure that we cannot get Roy off the case. May turn out to be a pain to both of us." Ketkar waited for a response from the other side. "Okay, if that is what you want. I will also try and see what I can do from my end," he said and disconnected the call.

A Story Two Decades Old

Roy picked Alina from the hotel at four in the evening. They drove to Lower Parel on his bike, preferring it over a cab in case they needed to make a quick exit. Roy drove slowly, carefully avoiding any sudden jerks, making sure to not give Alina any reasons to think he was being too wise.

In about an hour, they reached the chawl in which Babu had rented a room. The chawl was a three-storied rectangular structure surrounding a dusty courtyard. Each floor had multiple rooms with a common corridor connecting the rooms. Roy had come early as he wanted to search the room before Babu returned from office, hoping to find some evidence with which they could confront him when he came.

Roy and Alina asked for directions to Babu's place and were directed to a room on the second floor. They were greeted by a dilapidated door, which was secured with a rusted lock. "I will try to break in. You keep watch," Roy said. Alina turned her back to Roy to shield him from the neighbours.

Roy fished out a small pick and a tension wrench from his pocket. He inserted the pick in the upper pin of the key hole and brought his ears close to the lock – concentrating all his hearing abilities to the task. A smile escaped his lips as he heard a click. He had still not forgotten the trick he had learned at the orphanage. Roy inserted the wrench into the lower portion of the keyhole and swivelled it with a quick jerk. The lock gave away with a jolt.

Babu was munching on a bag of peanuts as he made his way home. It had not been a good day at office. He had been late for work, had burnt the tea, and had mixed so many files that he was asked to take the rest of the day off. Babu had noticed that his bosses were getting peeved at his behaviour, but he was not worried. He was a member of the workers' union and the company could do nothing more than issue a warning.

It was a small room that Babu stayed in – a mattress, a big steel chest and a line of drawers made up the entire furniture of the room. Roy searched the chest, while Alina rummaged through the drawers. They did not know what they were looking for and were just firing blank shots hoping to find something useful.

Roy could not see anything apart from soiled clothes and other small trinkets. Then his eyes fell on the makeshift attic towards the right. It was a bit high, and he could not make out whether there was anything kept on it. But if there was something Babu wanted to hide, then the spot seemed ideal for it.

With Alina's help, Roy moved the chest below the attic. He then stood over the chest, grabbed the outer edge of the attic and pulled himself up. "There are just pieces of paper strewn across," Roy said disappointed. "You keep looking in the drawers, while I'll try and see if anything here makes sense."

Alina meanwhile was making a thorough job of her search. She looked beneath clothes, past rolls of newspapers, rubbed her fingers over the linings to search for hidden compartments, doing all she could to throw more light on her mysterious stalker. It was in the last drawer, beneath a pile of keys, that she stumbled upon an old tinged photograph. She blew the dust off it and held it close to her eyes. There was no mistaking it – it was indeed Arun who was in the picture – posing on a scooter, with a shabby dark figure standing beside him. The photo was wrinkled and had yellowed at the edges. From Arun's face and untidy clothing, Alina could sense that the picture was at least a couple of decades old.

She was just about to direct Roy's attention to the picture, when she felt cold steel against her neck. "The guy in the picture looks familiar, doesn't he?" the voice holding the knife said. Alina had heard that chilling voice before and she did not have to turn around to know that it was Babu who stood behind her. He was pressing a foldable knife against her throat. "I did not know that I was going to be so lucky today," Babu said. "Let's see how you give me the slip this time." Alina was petrified, but at the same time she realised that Babu hadn't noticed Roy. She glanced towards the attic but could not see Roy from where she stood.

Babu made Alina stand up and walked her up towards the door – all the while, the knife pressed against her neck. "Go and shut the door," he said. "I would have not bothered your royal ass with such small chores if my hands were not preoccupied," he laughed, relishing having Alina at his mercy. She carefully shut the door, conscious of not making any swift movements. Babu then made her walk across the breadth of the room towards the steel trunk. He directed her to open the trunk and pulled out a bundle of rope. "Now, why don't you be a good girl and try and tie one end of the rope to this trunk," he said. Babu watched her as she tied the rope, occasionally checking the strength of the knot with his free hand. "You have done a fine job here. Looks like you enjoy being bound." He laughed again. "Sit down. Bring both your legs and hands together and daddy will tie you up real fine." Alina was calmly following instructions, reminding herself not to panic. She sat down, leaned forward and as instructed, brought her hands and feet together. Babu wrapped the rope around her hands and feet with his free hand, making several loops to ensure that she remained tightly bound. "Listen carefully now, I will let go of your neck to tie you a good knot. But don't do something stupid. I'd hate to ruin this beautiful face of yours," he sniggered.

Babu put aside the knife and bent forward to take hold of the rope. As soon as his hands moved away from Alina's neck, he heard a loud thud behind him. He turned just in time to see Roy's fist closing up on his face. Roy followed it up with another punch; this time hitting him smack on the nose. Before Babu could recover, Roy pulled out his pistol and held it right between Babu's eyes, Roy's fingers resting on the trigger. Within mere seconds, Roy had turned the situation on its head.

"I am sorry," Babu muttered, and kept repeating it like a kindergarten kid who had just been caught stealing candy. Roy picked him up by the collar and threw him in the corner, and then kicked at his ribs once more, angered at his audacity. "Now you listen to me," Roy shouted, his voice echoing in the small room, "I will unload all these bullets into your guts if you touch her again." Babu had suffered much to need any reminding. "We will ask you a few questions, and your only hope of salvation lies in you truthfully answering them." Babu nodded meekly.

"Is it Arun in this picture?" Alina asked, desperate to put this question before the others.

"Yes, that indeed is Arun," Babu said, wiping off the blood from his nose. "And the other person standing with him is my brother, Shankar. This photo was taken about twenty-five years back when both Arun and Shankar were studying together in Pali, a small Rajasthani village where both our families lived. They were best of friends, inseparable like only childhood friends can be."

Roy looked at Alina. "It is true that we come from Pali, but Arun has never mentioned anything about Shankar to me," she said.

"By the time you grew up, they had become strangers to each other," Babu said.

Alina and Roy looked at Babu suspiciously, not sure whether they wanted to believe his story.

"Arun became rich and my brother, the poor friend, was left behind." Babu picked himself up, leaning his back to the wall; this independently performed act gave him some strength to speak. "It is not that anyone can blame Arun for what happened. He worked zealously and deserved every penny of his pile." Babu gestured for a cigarette. Roy handed him one from his packet.

Babu took a puff, and then narrated his story. "Right from childhood, Arun, Shankar and I grew up together. Most of our waking hours used to be spent in each other's company, running around the school grounds, fighting in the sand or climbing up the little tree at the far end of the pond. Arun and Shankar were particularly close – him being more of a brother to Shankar than I ever was. In our early days, we were unfazed by the poverty of our families, but as the nonchalant childhood gave way to the restless teen years, we began to get aware of the miseries life bestows on poverty.

Slowly, but surely, steel entered Arun's hitherto careless soul. He was now possessed with a sense of determination, a strong will to wipe his life clean. He figured out that education was the only way to leave this wretched life behind. He started spending more and more time on his books. However, nothing changed for me and Shankar; we kept drifting along in our lives, taking each easy day as it came.

One day Arun asked us to join him in enrolling for an entrance exam to one of the prestigious colleges in Mumbai. Though me and Shankar knew that nothing would come off it for us, we accompanied him just to humour his wishes. Arun was of the view that it was hard to study for the exams while staying with our families, so all of us decided to spend a couple of months in a small village called Koregaon. One of Arun's relatives had an empty apartment there, and we figured we would be able to study there without any distractions.

"We spent a few months in Koregaon and then appeared for our exams in Mumbai, before returning to Pali." Babu hesitated for a moment, and his face turned a shade of white as if remembering those days were beginning to feel traumatic for him. "Things were not the same after that trip. There was an unspoken realisation between us that Arun was meant for bigger things than we were. Soon, Arun's parents also realised that the small town of Pali could not provide their son with the opportunities he sought. This was also the time when Arun's mother was about to give birth to Alina. They wanted her to have a better life than they had led, so Arun's family shifted to Mumbai. Shankar was heartbroken; he resolved to work harder and follow his friend to Mumbai. But there is a poisonous comfort to a life in a small town like ours. We soon settled back to our lazy routines, burning the ambitions of greatness in slow ambers of lethargy. Over the years, the physical and social gulf became too great for Arun to even acknowledge his friends of the past."

Alina listened to the story patiently. She knew from the bank statements that Arun continued to support Shankar, but did not yet want to broach the subject to Babu.

"Then about fifteen years back, Shankar and I decided to finally bid Pali adieu and came to Mumbai in search of opportunities. Neither did I ask, nor Shankar mentioned anything about approaching Arun for assistance in this big city. After a few months of struggle, I found a job as a clerk in a government office, while Shankar became a waiter in one of the fancy restaurants at Nariman Point. Then one day, by a cruel twist of fate, Arun walked into the very restaurant in which Shankar was employed.

Arun was with some of his friends, and was embarrassed to acknowledge Shankar in front of them. But later in the evening, he came back to seek Shankar out. Arun was clear that Shankar could not expect their friendship to rekindle, but he did promise to help Shankar out with a little bit of financial assistance. Last count I know, he was paying Shankar twenty grand a month as sustenance. This amount was enough for Shankar to quit his job and once again live a life of unemployed decadence. Fed by Arun's charity, he grew up to become a drunken sloth; whiling away his time in cheap bars, and reminiscing about old days to anyone who gave an ear."

"This is all fine," Roy was losing patience with Babu's story now. "But how does this all relate to you stalking Alina?" he asked.

"This is because four days back Shankar disappeared," Babu said in an exasperated tone. "At first I thought nothing of it. It was quite common for him to spend the night out on the streets in a drunken stupor, or to be picked up the police for bar room skirmishes. But then I read about Arun's death in the newspapers. I got convinced that this sounded too fishy to be a mere coincidence."

Babu sat up in attention, "My mind started racing. I checked out all the nearby bars and local police stations, but could not locate Shankar. At this point, I was exhausted and decided to approach you," he said pointing to Alina. "After all, you had also lost your brother and I naively hoped that you would be interested in helping me locate Shankar." Babu's voice could not hide the scorn he felt towards Alina. "But then at the Powai police station, I ran into one of my constable friends. He told me he had been assisting with Arun's investigation. I got interested and asked him to tell me more," Babu paused; unsure whether Roy would mind him saying anything more. But Roy signalled him to carry on. "My friend told me that the police was in no doubt that it was you who had killed Arun," Babu said. "This changed everything. I figured it was useless to approach you politely and instead made up my mind to track you down and scare you into telling me everything you knew. When I look back, it does seem like a stupid thing to do," he said with a sigh, "but you should make some concessions for the plight of a desperate brother."

The last sentence softened Alina a bit; the pain of losing Arun was still fresh in her mind. "I don't know anything about it," she said politely, but then hardened her voice. "And I daresay that I find it hard to believe your story completely. This all sounds a trifle fanciful."

"Well, I swear this is all there is to it," Babu said irritably. "And anyhow, you don't have to worry about me anymore. You have seen me and my place. I am sure you realise that I am no professional criminal, just an ordinary nobody driven by the love for one's family," he said, but at that moment Babu's jaws hardened, as if he had recollected something. "I am however sure you would not understand anything about a brother's love. I hope you get what is coming to you."

Roy had had enough of his blabbering. He propped up Babu by his collar. "For your own sake, I hope that all that you have said is true. I am going to leave you here for now, but if I hear anything funny about you, then I will pay you another visit, and this time it will be a lot worse." Roy scribbled something on a piece of paper and handed it over to Babu. "Here, this is my phone number and address. Contact me if you need to tell me anything more."

Just at this moment, Alina's mobile rang. "Hello Miss Ruia. We are calling from the Powai police station. We found out that you have checked out from the Renaissance Hotel and are not staying at your apartment either. So we were wondering where you are."

"I am still staying at the same hotel, but under a different name," Alina said. She considered telling them about this incident, but decided against it, "...as the press had been bothering me with their questions. Why do you ask?"

"Nothing specific, just keeping an eye on you. For your safety that is. I hope you understand."

"I do, and I want you to know that I am thankful for that," she said and hung up.

Roy and Alina rode back in despondent silence. The case had been getting knottier by the day, and the police were also losing their patience with Alina.

"Alina, I still have some questions for you," Roy said, as they reached the hotel. "Though I know that it is not a good time for you, I would appreciate it very much if we can get through them as soon as possible."

"I understand that," she gave it some thought. "Come up, we can discuss it in my room..."

In his chamber, Shantanu was thinking over the Roy problem. He had tried hard, but was unable to get Roy off the case. Exasperated, he decided to place a call to the headquarters. "Can I speak to Commissioner Sunil Dhawan please?" Shantanu said. The operator patched him through Sunil's line and after exchanging a few pleasantries, Shantanu came to the point.

"Sir, I have a small request I want you to consider," he said. "It is about this guy, Roy, whom you told us to assist on the case. I was wondering whether there is any chance of you reconsidering your decision." Shantanu heard what Sunil had to say patiently, not having any other option. "No, I understand that. It is just that he is proving to be a nuisance. My officers are complaining that he is always interfering in their work. And you do remember how we fired him for indiscipline. I am not sure he is someone we should allow to be in close contact to us." Shantanu was now getting irritated. "Yes, yes, I see. Yes sir, as you wish sir. Sure, that is how it will be." Shantanu hung up the phone in disgust. He was not sure what else could he do, but he knew he was running out of time.

Alina ordered two coffees and some sponge cake as soon as they reached the hotel. "Do you believe Babu's side of the story?" Roy asked.

"The monthly bank transfers...I have seen for myself. And it is true that my family is from Pali, but beyond that your guess is as good as mine," she snuggly tucked herself into bed. "So, you had some questions for me?"

"Yes, but I don't know how you will react," Roy said hesitatingly. "Would you mind telling me about your relations with your brother?" Roy asked almost apologetically.

But the question was not a surprise to Alina; she had always known that her relation with Arun would be the linchpin of any investigation. "Well, he was my brother," she said.

"That is one way of putting it," Roy said, indicating that he would need details.

"I actually hardly saw him when we were growing up. He was always out, striving to make a better life for himself," Alina said. "But that is not to say that I did not admire him. I loved him, waited for him to come home, talk to me, but he was never there for me. We were never close as siblings," Alina said and sat back against the bed. "Perhaps it was a reflection of the relationship that my father and mother shared. My father was not satisfied with a domestic life. He would go on long tours around the country, ostensibly to look for new business opportunities. But I think he wanted to just get away from all of us. And all through it, my mother suffered silently."

Alina was not talking only about Arun, but had subconsciously begun to peel layers of her entire childhood. These were the things that she had kept hidden inside her soul, but in the aftermath of Arun's death, all her repressed memories came pouring out. This was her silent outburst and it did not matter to her if anyone was listening. Roy lay back and let Alina talk to her heart's content.

"I knew my father detested my mother and always looked for an escape. Once Arun was born, my father took off; hardly ever returning home. On his part, he had given something to my mother to love and be busy with, and he did not want anything to do with her anymore. The only things my mother got were his money orders, accompanied by letters describing the wonderful places he was exploring. It was only towards the end of his youth that he returned from his travels. He acknowledged that he had not given my mother the marital bliss she deserved and decided to atone for the years spent away from her. I was the result of one his atonements."

She paused, as if pondering whether it would have been better if her father had never returned. All others had anyway died, leaving her alone to fight the battles. "This meant that Arun and I had a twenty-year age difference between us," she continued. "In such a situation, it was difficult for me to see a brother in him. On his part too, he took me to be his responsibility, always trying to improve me. He was irritated about my humped posture, not brushing after meals or noisily slurping my tea.

"I kept my distance from him; and even the few times I told him of things bothering me, instead of sympathy, I received wisdom. Always a sermon on how should a lady conduct herself and how it is the hardships that are the true test of one's character. He smothered me in a warp of accountability, and all this in the name of love." She looked upwards to the ceiling. "I think at some point in my childhood, I realised Arun towered over me – viewing himself as my saviour and that I was going to be scolded by him for revealing my insecurities. This walked with me into my maturity. I was always on my guard when in his company, careful not to reveal anything. Instead of siblings, we were two individuals staying together to share rent."

The room service came in with their coffee. Alina picked up a cup and blew at the froth. "The only one I was close to was my mother. I was ecstatic when she was happy and devastated when she was sad; it was as if the umbilical cord had never been cut. We both used to get together for a game of cards and convince each other, how lucky we were to have men as nice as father and Arun in our lives, too afraid of what breaking the illusion could do to us. It was clear to me that she felt neglected, but I could do nothing more than watch her wither away."

Alina paused for a while, and then wondered aloud, "I can no longer remember my mother's face. I know that she was a tall, dark lady with pouted lips and a slighting gait, but I cannot put all her features together. Sometimes I feel that I will get back my entire childhood if only I could remember her face." Suddenly she stopped, and seemed a bit lost. She looked towards Roy. "I think other people have more talent for living than I have. I have gained experiences and memories, but never truly lived. The only way I have responded to expectations is to sink further in my shell. It is difficult for me to emote as normal people do. I think I am saying these things for the first time, even to myself. But you are free to make any conclusions for your investigation."

Roy wanted to tell her it was all right to trust him. That he was not going to unfairly use anything she said. To tell her that he believed her innocence and would do anything to get her out. But he found it too trivial to paraphrase in words.

"And I also want to thank you for your help these past few days," Alina said. "It is difficult for me to approach anyone for assistance, but I am happy you offered without me asking."

Roy wanted to reach out and comfort her, to say that things would be fine. There was a period of silent admiration between them, which eventually morphed into a moment of awkwardness, until Alina filled it with words.

"I also want to assist in the investigation as much as I can. Whatever I have said, let it not lead you to conclude that I did not care for him. He was my only support and the only one whom I could call my own. You know, I did not even get to see his body after his death. Everything happened so suddenly that night. I was woken up by the police team and right after moved in to the hotel. I think because they thought of me as the suspect, they did not want me to hang around the scene for too long, so as to not allow me to interfere with anything. The police never informed me that they were done with the post mortem. But it was nice of Jayesh to call me and let me know before the cremation. He was very sympathetic of my situation. He said that it would be traumatic for me to see the body, especially after it had been mutilated during the autopsy. At the time, it seemed obvious to agree with him."

For the first time, Roy saw Alina's eyes welling up, but she wiped off the tears before they could crystallize. "I don't know how I will be able to repay Jayesh for all that he has done. He made sure that he was there to represent the family; otherwise it would have been a cremation in the presence of total strangers." She dabbed her eyes with the hotel towel. "Anyway, I want to do everything I can to help."

"I understand," Roy said. "I will let you know in case there is something you can help out with," he said, before he left the room.

The Man in the Uniform

Roy hummed along as he fixed his breakfast – a glass of juice and two pieces of toast. One of his old mates had remarked that he could always tell how happy Roy was by the amount of butter he put on his morning toast. Today, Roy was laying it thick. He grabbed his breakfast and went to sit by the side of the windowsill as he listened to the rain hitting the tin roofs. How wonderful it would have been if there was someone with him to share his meal; together they could look outside the window to try and make sense of the random beauty the city was. Roy could not fathom why he had felt this sudden pang for companionship. He had just begun trying to unravel the question, when his happy reverie was broken by the ringing of the door-bell. He peered through the peep hole. It was Babu standing outside. Roy looked closely. It did not appear as though Babu had any associates with him, but the tiny peep hole made it difficult to say it with certainty. It was a mighty stupid idea to give him my address, Roy thought. There was another press of the bell.

Roy ran a bit further back from the door and yelled, "Coming." Then he went about frantically searching for his pistol. He found it inside the trousers he had been wearing the day before. There was another press of the bell. Roy hid the gun behind his back, putting his right hand on the trigger and unlocked the door with his free hand. His movements were cautious, opening the door just enough to have a glance. But one look at Babu, and Roy realised that he need not have been so alarmed. Babu was standing there pale-faced, noticeably shocked and drenched in rain from head to toe.

"Be sure to lock the gate," Babu said as he entered the apartment, his voice quivering with fear.

Roy gave Babu a towel to dry himself, and a set of clothes to change into. They fitted loosely on Babu's short frame. Roy fixed Babu a cheese sandwich and a cup of coffee. He waited for Babu to drain down his cup.

"Do you want to tell me what happened?" Roy asked.

Babu spoke with perceptible urgency. "Last night after you guys left, someone knocked on my door. It was a person dressed in police clothes. I thought you and Alina were still angry at me, and had sent a policeman to straighten me out. He asked me to come with him to the station. I wanted to protest, to ask for a warrant, but his cold eyes told me that he was not much of a man for procedure. He put me on the back of the jeep –"

"Did you notice the number the jeep?" Roy asked, not patient enough for the tale to end.

"Do you look at the number plate of all the vehicles you get into"? Babu asked calmly, trying to hide his irritation.

"I sure do," Roy said. "But go on, I get your point."

"Well, for a good part of the journey, I thought he was driving me to the Powai police station. But a few minutes later, he took an unexpected turn. I figured that something fishy was going on, but did not dare open my mouth. You know, it does not augur well to be on wrong side of policemen. So I could only watch as he drove me deep into the Aarey Colony jungles, finally parking the car in a particularly secluded spot. He then told me he needed to take a piss, asking me to stay put. He left me in the jeep and walked about ten metres into the thicket." Babu paused for a big swig of water. "Sir, I am not a particularly intelligent man, but it does not take a particularly intelligent man to realise that something strange was going on. I was afraid of the policeman, but the fear for my life provided me the strength to disobey his command. I got down from the jeep and walked towards him, slouching behind the leaves. As I came closer, I could see him speaking to someone on the phone.

"'I have him,' he said. 'Where do you want him delivered?' He kept speaking on the phone, but I could not hear his words properly. So, I walked a bit closer. 'You sure you don't want me to finish him off right here? It would be pretty easy to hide the body in the forest," he was saying. 'No, I have not hurt him…yet.' You can imagine the effect these words had on my nerves. In those moments of carelessness, my foot apparently trampled on a frog. It croaked aloud, attracting the policeman's attention. He turned towards me, his eyes staring at me from between the leaves. Then I saw him pulling out his gun from the holster. I dashed away, panicking. As far as I can recall, I did not hear any gunshots, so probably he did not think it wise to kill me there. But obviously, I did not turn back to find out."

Roy got up and walked towards the window. The rain had stopped, leaving muddy streets behind. "Has anything of this sort happened to you before?" he asked.

"No sir."

"And about Shankar's disappearance...did you tell this man about it?"

"No, it was only you and Alina who know."

"I don't like the sound of this. First Shankar goes missing, then Arun gets murdered and now you come here with this fine story." Roy shoved his breakfast aside, and lit up a cigarette. "Whoever is behind all this is resourceful. It's quite possible that he would know about me and my flat as well, which is going to make it dangerous for you to stay here. Returning back to your quarters is out of question. What we need is a safe accommodation for you to hide, and I think I know just the person who might have a house or two to spare." Roy fetched his phone and dialled Jayesh's number.

Ketkar and Romil were hurtling towards Shantanu's chamber for a catch up. In the very first week of joining, Ketkar had told Romil of the Shantanu catch up, which he began by discussing the case under investigation and then lorded over a dressing down session, in which the subordinates were painfully made aware of how slow and stupid they had been while conducting the inquiry.

Shantanu politely asked Ketkar and Romil to take the chairs, while he read the morning business papers. After making sure they had waited for a quarter of an hour, he delicately folded the paper and directed his gaze upon them. "I have never understood the stock market, you know. Makes a mockery of the real world." Romil looked nonplussed. He could not figure out whether Shantanu had invited them over to discuss stocks or their work.

"It's simple really," he blurted out. "I will give you a book that explains everything in simple terms." Ketkar did well to suppress a laugh, but Shantanu did not look amused.

"Gentlemen, I have called you to discuss the Arun murder case. Any updates?" he asked.

"We have taken the interviews of all parties concerned and...," Ketkar began.

"That was a day's work," Shantanu interjected. "Anything post that?"

Romil said, "Sir, we are trying..."

"You keep quiet," Shantanu snapped. "Don't speak out of turn." Romil sunk back in his chair like a child who had just been scolded for spilling his milk. Shantanu looked at Ketkar with a look that said, from one man to another. "Ketkar, there is a lot of media interest in this murder. They have been hounding me for details ever since the story broke out. I want a few arrests to show that we have been working."

"I get it, sir. But the only real lead we have is his sister. And the evidence against her is only circumstantial. I was hoping for the forensics team to come up with something to help us, but they have drawn a blank."

Shantanu furrowed his brow; Ketkar never missed a chance to make Roy's absence felt. "Work with what you have. I don't expect a person of your calibre to come up with such flimsy excuses. I want some arrests, and I want them quick. This does not mean that you go around and put just anybody behind the bars. I want you to get your hands on some real evidence before you proceed."

"We will try our best," Ketkar said as Romil and he walked out of Shantanu's chamber.

Roy and Babu sat patiently, waiting for their host to speak. Jayesh was reclined on his couch, staring at the problem that had landed up so suddenly at his doorstep. "There is a guest house I have, on the outskirts of Lonavala. It is in a small clearing in the middle of the forest, pretty secluded from the rest of the city. I try and go there at least once a month to clear my thoughts. As I see, it should be perfect for your purposes." Babu was elated at Jayesh's offer. "That is more than I could have hoped for," he said, feeling grateful.

"I will have the place ready and ask the caretaker to go on leave, so that there is no one to bother you. Have you had lunch?" he asked Babu. Then without waiting for an answer, he told Babu to head for the conference room on the left, where someone would arrive with his food. Jayesh waited for Babu to get out.

"Don't make me more involved in this than I need to," he said to Roy. "I am taking him in, but what if the police find out. You told me that the man chasing him was dressed as a cop. What if he was a real one?"

"I understand your predicament," Roy said. "But it's difficult for me to arrange a suitable place for Babu. We can of course let him fend on his own, but I am not sure how long he'd be able to survive."

"Okay, I put my trust in you when I hired you," Jayesh said. "And now I can do nothing but just hope that you know what you are doing." He picked up the phone and placed a call to the caretaker of the guest house. "Hello Prasad, I will be arriving today in a few hours. I will like some seclusion while I am there, so please clean up the place and take a few days off. I don't know how long I will be staying, so you don't need to come back till you receive a call from me." He hung up and turned to Roy. "If you don't mind, I want to leave right away. I have a relatively free schedule today and want to be done with this as soon as possible." Jayesh next called his driver, "Please bring the car to the entrance. Make sure that the tank is full and leave for the day." He also phoned his secretary to cancel all his meetings. "There you go Roy, everything settled." Roy could not help feeling impressed with the efficiency with which Jayesh took care of his affairs.

Within twenty minutes, Jayesh, Babu and Roy were in the car, driving to Lonavala. It took them a good part of the hour to get out of the city traffic and hit the highway. Jayesh rolled down his windows, and pushed the accelerator to the maximum, clearly enjoying his time out of office. "It's been a while since I have been out for a long drive," he shouted towards Roy, struggling to get himself heard over the wind. "If you don't mind, I will stop over for some tea," he said pulling up at a roadside eatery. Babu got out to order tea and snacks for them, while Jayesh and Roy strolled along to the edge of the road, admiring the view of the hills.

"I feel stuck in that office sometimes, you know," Jayesh said.

"Have you thought of leaving city life and moving somewhere quieter, may be to this guest house of yours?" Roy asked.

"Success demands its own price, Roy," Jayesh said. "It's difficult for me to leave the firm I have built myself from scratch. I would never be able to forgive myself if someone comes and ruins the place. I had been looking at Arun as a possible successor, but I don't know what to do now." He walked off towards the hill. "I have a lot of memories of the city, mostly pleasant ones and it is only the past memories and relations that keeps one alive at this age of life. I don't want to leave them behind." He kicked a stone down the hill, and watched it as it slowly tumbled into the abyss below. "It's strange but I had never imagined myself getting old. It feels like I have already lived out my entire share of experiences. Whatever I do now, just seems to be a cheap copy of the life I already drank." Jayesh smiled and looked at Roy. "Just one thing more to do, and then I will be ready to kick the bucket."

After refreshments, they headed back to the car. Jayesh asked Roy for the keys. "I don't have them," Roy said, with a confused face. They looked at Babu, but he too conveyed ignorance. They threw polite accusations at each other to try and ascertain who held the keys last; and then unsuccessfully searched for them at the restaurant. Luckily, one of the back doors was still unlocked, and they could at least get into the car.

"Well, this is a sweet problem. It would be difficult to get any cabs on the highway," Roy said.

"Let me try something," Jayesh said cheekily. He got into the driver's seat and stretched his hands beneath the steering column and tussled with a tangle of wires. He then fused three of the wires together and scraped them against a fourth. The engine started with a whirring sound.

"How do you know all this? I am suddenly suspicious of you," Roy said with a chuckle. But one look at Jayesh, and Roy realised that he had not found the joke funny.

It took them another hour to reach their destination. Jayesh parked the car a good hundred meters away from the compound. "You guys go ahead," he said. "If you don't mind, I am going to play this thing from a distance. Babu, you will find the keys beneath the doormat."

Jayesh pulled out a few thousand rupee notes and handed them to Babu. "You can get your food from the market which is about a kilometre to the left." Babu took the notes and tucked them carefully inside his trouser pocket. "One more thing," Jayesh said. "I have got motion detectors installed around the perimeter, so you will know if anyone approaches the place. The detectors are connected to a wireless beeper which you will find in the living room drawer. And take this…" he fished out his visiting card from the wallet. "If you need anything, call me."

Roy and Babu proceeded to the guest house. Roy noticed that there were two locks on the door. He looked around and caught sight of a palm sized stone. He picked up the stone and smashed it across the second lock. He kept striking it, until the lock splintered out of the door.

"Jayesh wanted me to make this look like a break-in," Roy said to Babu. "If something funny happens around here, then this will give him an excuse to deny all knowledge of the matter." It's all about laying layers between the problem and oneself, like the old man likes to say."

Babu let out a feeble whistle. "The old man would have made one smart crook."

After taking a brief tour of the house, Roy left Babu to his small kingdom, while he and Jayesh drove back to Mumbai. Roy could not recall at what point exactly did the conversation veer towards Alina, but he found Jayesh taking an uncanny interest in Roy's and Alina's blossoming friendship.

"Do you have a thing for her?" Jayesh suddenly asked.

Roy was taken aback. This was a question he had been reluctant to even ask himself. Jayesh could make out that Roy was getting uncomfortable. "Ah, I should have probably not asked that. Your personal life is none of my business." Roy was relieved when Jayesh dropped the subject. He thanked Jayesh for helping out with Babu and promised to keep him updated about the case.

Roy decided to spend the evening couched up in his apartment, looking over the photocopies of the case files. He took them out of the cupboard and stacked them up on the dining table. He fixed up a large peg of brandy and laid a packet of cigarettes on the table, all set for a long night of work.

The Legend of the Kadera

Roy woke up on his chair, slumped backwards with his arms to his side. The window was open and the case papers had been blown all over the room. Roy grudgingly picked, sorted and tied them up into a bundle. He washed his mouth with some stale coffee and then sat over the pages again, casually flipping them over. The fingers stopped at the section he had highlighted the previous night.

The forensics team had found the body on the bed, and Arun's shotgun lying close to his legs. The only wound on his body was that of the gunshot, piercing right through the abdomen. Studying the wound on the body and the firing capabilities of the gun, the forensics team had estimated that the bullet was fired at a distance of roughly two feet from the body. Reads out a normal scene of crime – gun, bullet, wound – all in place, Roy thought. But he still could not see how someone might have entered the building, floated through the main door without breaking the lock, killed Arun and then got away without a trace. Yet he was not ready to believe that Alina could have murdered Arun. However, going forward, he decided to be careful of how much he told her about the investigation.

Roy looked over the photographs of Arun's body and his face. No one would have said that this photograph and the photograph Roy had seen at Babu's place were of the same person. Twenty years and a bagful of money had made Arun a lot fatter and fairer. Roy was particularly interested in the photos of the close ups of the wound, going over them again and again. There was something that stuck out like a sore thumb, though he was at a loss to pinpoint what exactly.

Exasperated, he set aside the papers and stepped into the shower, letting the cold water run all over him. This was probably the first time since getting Chandra's call that morning that Roy had felt free to spend some time on himself in peace. The case had been taking a toll on him with its knotting complexities on the one hand and his yet unacknowledged affection for Alina on the other. His pleasant thoughts were broken by the shrill sound of the doorbell. Roy grudgingly wrapped a towel around his manhood and stepped out to answer the door. He saw that an unmarked brown envelope lay near the entrance – apparently slipped under the door.

He picked up the envelope and slit open the letter inside. It took him only one glance to determine that the sender had gone to great pains to conceal his identity. Both the envelope and the letter were of standard size and type – the most easily available specimens at the local stores. The few lines written across it were traced using an alphabetic stencil. The letter was made up of a single paragraph, and titled *'The Legend of the Kadera'*. The heading had sufficiently piqued his interest, and he at once went about reading the contents:

The Legend of the Kadera

Long before history began, there stood a remote village atop a volcanic plateau in the island kingdom of Japan. It was an unremarkable village, save for the presence of an old white bearded monk who lived alone at the far end of the village. The simple-minded village folks were suspicious of the monk and would have long chased him away if not for the popular legend that he was the last surviving 'kadera' *– the ancient warriors capable of bending arrows. Then one day, when the clouds were quiet and the wind was silent, the village was attacked by a Waira, the bison beast. The Waira chopped the women and ate up the children, and men ran amok in fear. It was at this instant that the monk – the last living arrow bender – approached the beast, a bow in his hand and one single arrow in his quiver. The beast picked up a huge boulder and charged towards the monk. The monk stood erect, planted his foot in the volcanic mud and placed an arrow on his bow, pointed straight at the boulder. It was something in the eyes of the monk that made the beast stop midway in his tracks; he felt too afraid to go anywhere near his old, withered challenger of his. Instead, the beast gathered up all his strength and hurled the boulder at the monk. The villagers expected the monk to run away, but he stood still, watching the boulder soar towards him. Only a fraction of a moment before the boulder crushed the monk, did the villagers see the arrow fly away from his bow. And they saw the arrow angling away past the boulder and then they saw it bending around it, hitting the beast right between his eyes. This, the Japanese say, was the story of the last kadera – the last arrow bender. The arrows have since then, forever flown straight.*

The letter was signed, *'From someone who has seen the arrows fly'*.

Roy was at a loss. He could make no sense of the letter, yet it was too carefully crafted to be a silly joke. He sat down on the chair, and lit a cigarette, going over the letter's contents again. He then went back and had a second look at the photographs of Arun's apartment. It was then that something caught his eye. He jumped up and rushed towards the door. If Roy understood what the letter was trying to say, then there was no time to waste.

Romil was still on his way to office when he received the call. "Yes Roy, I will be there right away," he said. "No, don't worry. I will not be late." It had been raining heavily and Romil had to pay the auto rickshaw driver something extra to get him to change direction and head towards Hiranandani. He found Roy waiting for him at the gate of Arun's apartment.

"I appreciate you coming at such short notice," Roy said. Romil was embarrassed on being thanked; he was more used to orders than requests. "I don't mind at all. What do you need me for?" he asked.

"There is something that I wanted to check," Roy said. "But I am not allowed to enter the flat without a police escort."

Romil saw that Roy had brought along with him a dozen or so long plastic tubes and a life-sized mannequin. The mannequin had a big hole untidily drilled through the abdomen; clearly a job done in a hurry. "What are these for?" Romil asked as they entered the apartment.

"Forget about these for a moment, and let us go over the sequence of events of that night once more," Roy said. "Alina comes home at midnight, and gets into the apartment using her key. She then locks the apartment door from the inside, and goes straight to her room, which is right next to the gate of the apartment," Roy said, pointing to her room. "She claims that after entering the flat, she ate her dinner and went straight to bed, without entering Arun's room. Now, two-and-a half hours later, at about 3:45 a.m., the neighbours hear a gunshot, and they phone the police. The police station is close by, and they arrive within fifteen minutes of hearing the shot. They find that the front door is locked. So they ring the bell, and when no one answers the door, they pry it open using an iron bar. Do you agree with the sequence of events Romil?" Roy asked.

"Yes, that is how it was," Romil replied confidently.

"Great then, also remember that there is a CCTV camera at the building gate. It was functioning all the while and as per the security guard's testimony, did not record any strangers coming in or going out of the building. Putting all these pieces together, it seems that someone came in at 3:45 a.m. undetected by the cameras and magically got inside the apartment. He or she then murdered Arun using his own shotgun and went out of the apartment while managing to lock the gate from inside. What does it all point to?"

"This is not possible," Romil said enthusiastically. "It could only be that Alina is lying and she is the killer..."

Roy laughed. This is not what he was trying to direct Romil to. "Yes, that is a possibility," he said. "But then there is another probability," he waited for a few seconds for Romil's response, but looking at his confused expression said, "What if the killer did not leave the apartment that night?"

"But the police made a thorough search of the place. They could not find anyone?" Romil said.

"That is because they did not know where to look," Roy said.

Romil was having difficulty in making sense of what Roy was saying, and instead of questioning him, found it better to simply observe whatever Roy was up to. Roy led him to Arun's room.

"Let me give you a small demonstration," Roy said. "Can you do me a favour and count the number of bullet marks you see on the back wall of the room?"

Romil obediently tallied them. "I can count about seven marks," Romil said. "But why are there so many marks when only one bang was heard?" He sounded irritated with himself on having overlooked such a simple fact earlier.

"You will need some knowledge of shotguns to understand this," Roy said. "You see, a shotgun fires in a very different way than an ordinary gun. While a simple pistol fires a single intact bullet, a shotgun bullet or a shell as it is called, has many small fragments called pellets packed inside them. So when a shotgun shell is fired, it releases all those pellets at one go."

"So, you are saying that when a shotgun is fired, then instead of a single bullet, a bunch of bullets are shot at once?"

"Yes, exactly," Roy said. "This is why shotguns are such deadly weapons for close range combats. They knock down their target even if the shooter does not exactly hit its aim. In our case, this particular shotgun shell had nine pellets packed into it. And so you should not be surprised to see up to nine pellet marks on the wall. The rest of the two pellets must have stayed lodged inside the victim's body…"

"I see – one shell and nine pellets," Romil said, jotting everything down in his notebook.

"Now tell me, do you see anything strange about the positioning of these pellet marks on the wall?" Roy asked like a teacher questioning his student.

Romil stared carefully. "Nothing that I can make out."

"It's not your fault. The thing is not obvious to the naked eye. But let me arrange a small experiment for you," Roy said. "Lend me a hand with the dummy." They picked up the dummy and made it to stand just beside the foot of the bed.

"As per the police's crime scene reconstruction, this is the point at which Arun must have been standing when he was shot from a distance of roughly two feet away," Roy said. "Now you go and stand two feet in front of the dummy, the point at which the bullet was supposedly fired from."

Romil went and stood at the indicated spot. "Let us try and trace the path of the pellets," Roy said. "The pellets were fired from the point at which you were standing…then they passed through Arun's abdomen and hit the back wall – all in a straight direction – because you know that bullets are just like arrows and cannot bend," Roy said with a mysterious smile.

Once Romil stood at the spot, Roy asked him to hold one of the plastic tubes that he had brought along. Romil held one end of the tube with his hand at the position at which a person of average height would be holding a gun, while Roy took the other end of the tube. Roy then passed the tube through the abdomen of the dummy where the hole was drilled. He then laid this end of the tube against the back wall. He marked the spot at which the tube touched the wall with an X." Then he did the same with eight more tubes, resulting in a tight cluster of nine X marks on the back wall.

Romil saw that this X marked cluster was at a much lower point than the actual bullet marks. And even when he tried to adjust his position in various ways to reconcile with the police theory, there seemed no way in which the pellets could have hit the actual marks that were on the wall.

"What you see indicated by the Xs is the potential area over which the bullet marks would have spread in case they were fired from the spot where you are standing. But the actual bullet marks are much higher than these points. So there is no way the killer would have fired that shot standing at the position that you are," Roy said, confirming Romil's suspicion. "Now, let us conduct one more demonstration."

This time Roy asked Romil to place the dummy on the bed in a sitting position, in the exact spot where Arun's body was found. Romil knew that he was watching a master at work but was too occupied in the experiment to say anything. Roy meanwhile bent the dummy forward and stretched its hand as far forward as possible so that the hands reached just about the edge of the bed. He then asked Romil to hold the tubes at the point till where the dummy's hands were. As done for the previous experiment, he passed the tubes through the abdomen, and then touched them against the wall. This time, the touch points corresponded exactly to the actual bullet marks.

"Do you mean to say that it was Arun himself who reached for the trigger of the shotgun and killed himself with the barrel pointed upwards to his abdomen?" a shocked Romil asked.

"I am not saying anything Romil," Roy said with a smile. "It is the evidence which says so. And evidence does not lie, does not bend, and does not succumb to influence." But Romil was unconvinced; it was difficult for him to let go of the many theories he had been forming.

"And there is one more thing," Roy said sensing Romil's indecision. "When shotgun the pellets are put into their shell, then along with the pellets, a white powdery substance called grex is also packed in. This powder is necessary for the pellets to retain their spherical shape when they are fired at such high pressure and velocity. If Arun would have been fired at from the distance that is supposed by the police, then this white powder would have been found spread all around Arun's clothes. But when I looked at the photographs of Arun's wound, there was no presence of the white powder on his shirt. But the autopsy report confirms that there was a lot of that powder on the inside of his shirt, right around and inside the wound." Roy paused for a moment to let Romil understand the full import of what he was saying. "And this points to only one direction – the gun was pressed tightly against Arun's abdomen when it was shot and not from a distance of two feet."

"This is incredible," Romil said with a tremendous sense of disbelief. It was only now that Romil understood what Roy meant when he said that the killer had not left the apartment that night. "And you found all this by just looking at the photographs? The forensics team with all the resources and all the time drew a blank." He excitedly said, "I will go and inform Ketkar sir right away." And he ran out of the door even before Roy could have a chance to ask for help to carry the dummy back.

Ketkar was just about to knock on Shantanu's cabin when he heard voices inside. The subject of the conversation froze his steps.

"You have to keep an eye on him," Shantanu was saying. "Track his movements and identify the people he visits – anything that you can find. It would be a disaster if we don't get to know what he is up to."

"But it is not like I control him," the other person in the office said. "I don't know half the places he goes to."

"I understand your problem, but you must know that you are my only hope. I had put Ketkar on the task, but I am not happy with his progress. I sometimes get the feeling that Ketkar is trying to help *him* rather than me. This is the reason why I want you to have a go at it. Please do everything that is possible for you, and report to me if you find anything."

Ketkar was finding it uncomfortable to stand in the corridor. It was a busy office, and he would be in trouble if anyone found him outside Shantanu's cabin with his ears against the door. He knocked twice.

"Come in!" Shantanu's voice boomed.

Ketkar walked in to find Chandra sitting along with Shantanu. He tried hard to behave normally.

"I have called Chandra for an update on the case," Shantanu said without being asked for an explanation, his guilt making him justify Chandra's presence.

Ketkar acknowledged Chandra with a half-hearted smile, and then turned to Shantanu. "Sir, I have something urgent to discuss. It will be best if we spoke in private."

Chandra got up from the chair even without Shantanu asking him to.

Shantanu looked apologetically at Chandra, walked him out of the door and then gave a cold stare at Ketkar. "Tell me what is it that could not keep you waiting till the end of my meeting?" he said gruffly.

"Romil escorted Roy to Arun's apartment, where he conducted a few experiments," Shantanu stopped fiddling with his phone and looked at Ketkar. Ketkar knew he now had Shantanu's attention. "Roy has informed me that Arun's death might have been a suicide."

Shantanu wiped his face with his hands to make a display of his frustration, "I don't know why all of you are so obsessed with what Roy is saying or doing. He may come up with as many fanciful theories as he wants. Nothing of that should influence our investigation," he said.

"Romil was saying that Roy made a pretty convincing case; backed by ample evidence," Ketkar pleaded.

"It's easy to make Romil believe in anything one wants," Shantanu retorted. But then, sensing that he was sounding too dismissive, he added, "Do one thing. Go over the files again. Also, check the previous case reports. See if there are any parallels that you can draw with this case. And give me something by tomorrow morning."

"But that will take time. I will have to go through similar cases one by one, and check the medical possibilities to see if what he is saying is feasible. I will have to spend the entire night going over the reports if I am to give you something by tomorrow," Ketkar protested, wondering whether this was punishment for interrupting Shantanu's meeting with Chandra.

Shantanu removed his glasses and placed them on the desk, and then bent forward to meet Ketkar's eyes, "So, what is your point?" he asked with a grimace.

"Nothing, I guess I will get going right away then," Ketkar said, feeling like a lamb being led to the butcher.

The Morning After

Roy was not sure how to break the fact about Arun's suicide to Alina. It would have been a better idea to give her a few days to get over his death; but then, he also had to find out if there was anything that had been bothering Arun. All of a sudden, Alina felt as much a stranger as when Roy had first called her at the hotel.

With a heavy hand, he rang the bell of her room. She responded from inside the room, but kept him waiting out in the corridor. When she opened the door, he saw that she had taken the time to fix up her hair, and to put a fresh coat of gloss. The dark patches around her eyes had reduced from the time he last saw her, and her fancy pink shirt told him that she felt good enough to be taking an interest in her clothes again. Walking into the room, he felt like a criminal about to commit a murder.

Not knowing what to do next, he went up to the jug and filled up a glass of water. This one solemn act was enough for Alina's female sensitivity to know that something was amiss, and she immediately draped herself in a formal demeanour. "So, what is it?" she asked.

"Alina, it's…," Roy stopped, realizing that his voice was trembling. Almost intuitively, he reached out and held her by the shoulders. "I think Arun committed suicide," he said it in one go. Alina maintained her countenance, though he could feel her voice sounded restrained. "Are you sure of it?" she asked.

"Well, as much as I can tell by the evidence, but I may have missed something," he felt compelled to not attach any finality to his theory. She sat down on the sofa and began fiddling with her phone. He saw in her the poise that the police team had found so incriminating, but he could also see that she was just trying to keep her fingers busy and her mind occupied.

"So, what do you want now?" she asked without glancing at him.

He took a seat on the bed, wanting to give her as much physical space as she wanted. "Anything you think that may have been bothering him? He might have been sick or had made a trade that went bad?" Roy knew it was an insensitive question, but he wanted to keep Alina's mind occupied.

"Nothing that he told me," the anger, stoked by the brother's love, simmering in her voice.

"Maybe it was something he was personally suffering from. Something he did not want you to get hurt about." She nodded her head, in a way that indicated her acknowledging that she had heard it, rather than putting any faith in Roy's conjectures.

Sitting there quietly in the room, Roy was starting to get uncomfortable. He did not have anything to say and nothing with which he could break the deadlock. But he also knew that Alina's silence had been crying for company, and he could not leave her alone.

Alina set aside the phone and looked at Roy. Her eyes were filled with water, but had not yet given her tears the permission to flow. She got up from the sofa, and came and sat beside him on the bed. "Maybe I could have done something about it," she said in a chocking voice. "I ignored the fact that I was the only one in his life. He might have craved for companionship as much as I did. And now when all this has happened, I feel so guilty to have done nothing to break the walls that we created between ourselves." At the time, hugging Alina seemed the most natural thing for Roy to do. Roy had always wanted Alina to be as close to him as she now was. But at this moment, all he could picture was Arun sitting alone in his house, and deciding that he had nothing and no one to live for. He felt sorry for the man who had achieved everything he wanted and then realised that like everyone else, all he had ever wanted was love.

Alina looked into Roy's eyes, and drew him closer. She took his lower lip into her own. Roy was not sure how to react. He saw this as Alina's susceptibility and did not want to do anything to hurt her at this emotional juncture. But he did not find in him the courage to push her away. "Don't think you are doing anything wrong," Alina said, sensing Roy's awkwardness. "I have had it on my mind for a while, and I need this now." Roy looked at her. She seemed overcome by pain; her face burning with a passion deep and crimson. Even if he knew Alina was not being completely honest to him, Roy convinced himself that it was the truth. His arms eased around her and he took her lips into his.

Roy was the first to wake up. He got out of the bed and walked towards the window. The sun was shining brightly into the lake, reflecting its splendour back on Roy's face. It is the morning that is the preserver of judgement and holds a mirror to the errors of fancy which are committed in the night, he thought. Roy felt guilty of having let himself flow with the moment, but then one look at Alina's face and all his pangs of regret were cleansed away. As she lay there sleeping, he realised that she was much more beautiful than even his memory of her, so splendidly did she glow in the sunlight.

Alina woke up to the sight of Roy standing at the window, staring at her. She smiled at him, and waved at him to come and sit by her side. "It has been difficult for me to trust people," she said wrapping herself around his chest. "There was one before you too, you know."

"I don't care for such things," Roy said.

"But I want to be completely honest with you before we start something," she said. "I have done things I am not proud of."

Roy brought Alina's face up to meet his, but she turned them back down as if such matters were best discussed with both pairs of eyes turned away. "He was five years older to me, and I didn't know that he was married when I started seeing him. By the time I found out, I was already addicted to him like an old spinster to her cheap scent of perfume. I remember it all like one long torment, but that was also in a way part of my addiction. It ended as abruptly as it had begun." Alina hugged him tighter to convince herself that Roy was dear enough to part with her history.

"Once we rented a cottage in one of the secluded places in Goa," Alina said. "It was March and it seemed we were all alone on the beach. He had gone into the town to get some alcohol, so I went to the beach on my own. I was lying down on the sand when I noticed a girl swimming from another beach towards me. She emerged out of the water completely naked and lay down beside me. She told me that her name was Hilda and she was from Germany. Egged on by her, I too took off my top and we both lay there sunbathing, feeling completely free, enjoying the bountiful nature as it was meant to be.

"Suddenly I saw two boys hopping around on the rocks above us, stealthily peeking at us. 'Let them look, they are too young...completely harmless,' Hilda said, and closed her eyes again. My first reaction was to jump towards my top, but then I calmed myself down and lay there with my front in complete view.

"I noticed the boys starting to come closer. They stood there, just staring at us. Then the more daring of the two came closer to Hilda, bending down as if looking for shells. I felt so strange and then suddenly Hilda said to the boy, 'Are you just going to watch or do you plan on coming closer?'

"He hastily undid his clothes and in no time was on top of her. He jumped around her like a hungry maniac and she giggled all through it, letting him play around with her breasts and her lips. The other boy kept staring from a distance. Hilda guided the boy into her, and he came down on her. They were so close to me that the air from the boy's breathe hit my face.

"I don't know what happened, but I suddenly turned to the boy and said, "Aren't you coming over me too?" Hilda took him out and passed her toy over to me. He hopped over to me and held me by my breasts. It hurt so bad. He arched his back and came all over me. It was then that from the corner of my eye, I saw my man standing at a distance with a bottle in his hand, watching me. There was disgust in his eyes; a verdict that they delivered. But I could not care less. I was at last feeling free. I looked away from him and hugged the boy close," Alina abruptly stopped. Roy could feel the moisture from Alina's tears saturating through the sheet. "Ever since that day, I have been ashamed of myself. I see the guilt in me through his eyes. Never have I been able to come close to anyone again," she finally lifted her head and looked at Roy, her soul asking for forgiveness now that she had confessed. Roy merely took her hands into his and caressed them, his touch letting her know that there was nothing to be sorry for, and he loved and cared for her for all that she was. A part of him was relieved that she was not perfect, that he could still hope to hold on to her for the rest of his life.

They took a shower and sat together for breakfast. "Listen, I was thinking about what you told me last night...about something bothering Arun," Alina said. "Now that I come to think of it, Arun had mentioned a couple of times that he had been to the doctor right before it all happened. Though I did not see anything unusual about that, I just thought you would want to know."

"Did he say whom did he visit?" Roy asked.

"He did not say that; but in all probability it would be Dr. Kapoor, our family physician. He works in the Hiranandani Hospital. If you want, I can introduce you to him."

"That sounds good," Roy said, applying a thick layer of butter on his toast. "Let him know that I will be visiting him tomorrow."

"But he will not be available tomorrow. He is there on alternate days. It would be better if you go and see him today itself."

"But today will not be possible for me. I was planning a quick trip to Pali."

"Pali? Why do you have to go to Pali?" Alina asked surprised.

Roy had not wanted to refer to the letter, but it was not possible to get out of this direct question. "There are things that I need to look into," he said, pulling out the document from his pocket. "This is the letter that was delivered to me some time back," he flattened the sheet on the bed. "But I still don't know who wrote this." Alina began reading the contents at once. "And if you observe carefully," Roy said, "… the writer signs off saying that he had seen the arrows fly. I don't know what this means; whether he is claiming that he was in Arun's room that night or I am simply reading too much into it. Whatever it is, we cannot sit back until we know everything about the case."

"Hmm, I see your point. But this letter does not mention anything about the author apart from that line at the end. How will you ever go about locating him?"

"I am not sure," Roy said, scratching his forehead. "But looking into Shankar's disappearance and the attack on Babu seem to be the most obvious way to go forward. I want to go to Pali to check out Babu's story, and see if I can find something else about those two there. But with this doctor thing today, guess I'll have to postpone those plans."

"Why don't I go to Pali?" Alina said after some thought. "I still know a few relatives there. Would be a lot easier for me to locate Shankar and Babu's family and verify his side of things."

Roy thought for a while. It was true that it would be much easier for Alina to find her way around Pali, and he could really do with unloading some of the weight on his back. "That would be great," he said, "But are you sure you want to do this?"

"Yes, I want to," she said with the kind of strength that can only be brought together with grief.

"That is settled then," Roy said. "I will make all the arrangements. You catch the next flight to Jodhpur. A car will be waiting to take you to Pali." He looked at his watch, and smiled. "We still have a couple of hours before your flight. And since today is a special day, I want to take you somewhere."

"But what is so special about today?"

"Because it comes only once in a year," Roy said, not wanting to reveal more.

"At least tell me whether I should wear something special?" Alina asked, still wrapped in the sheets.

"Just wear something," Roy said laughing, right before Alina threw her pillow at his face.

Sewri dockyard was located in the older parts of the city; the entire area was lined with slums from the dockyards to the sea. The lanes turned narrower as Roy's bike moved closer to the sea. The houses were smaller and darker; the streets were dirty as days of waste lay in pools on either side of the narrow path.

Roy parked the bike, and led Alina into what was essentially a big hole blasted through a brick wall. Inside, they came to an old courtyard which seemed to be in need of constant repairs. At one end of the courtyard, there was a steep narrow stairway; while at the other three, metal workers were pounding on a slab of iron. A fire burned behind them, casting an orange glow, that pushed its way between them, lighting up their faces. Roy led Alina straight up the stairway.

At the end of the climb, they came across a small door with a rusted horse shoe handle guarding the entrance. Roy's knock was answered by a few coughs and the sound of a pair of legs slowly dragging themselves across the floor. The door creaked open, and in front of them stood an old, petite man; his short stature accentuated by a pronounced hunch of the back.

A smile spread across the old man's face as soon as he saw Roy. "I knew you would come," he said hugging Roy in a light embrace. Then his eyes fell on Alina. He put on the glasses that were suspended with a thread across his neck. "So, you got a new one this time," he said in dull matter of fact voice. Both Roy and Alina could not help but let out a chuckle.

He welcomed them in his small, but well lit shanty and offered a seat on the bed – the only piece of furniture in the room. "Wait here, I will get your gift," the old man said and disappeared behind a set of curtains.

"What gift is he talking about?" Alina asked.

"My birthday gift of course," Roy said, with a childish delight on his face.

Before Alina could react to the news, the man came back with a small parcel wrapped in a gift paper. He stood and watched as Roy delicately unwrapped the parcel, careful not to damage the paper. "Ah, my favourite chocolate, Cadbury's Dairy Milk!" exclaimed Roy.

"He is just feigning surprise, dear," the old man said to Alina. "He gets the same gift every year."

"This is because it is the best thing Sehdev Kaku," Roy said, tightly wrapping the old man in his arms. "Did anyone else come this year?"

"No son," the old man said. "They stopped coming long back," he came and sat beside Roy. "But I have no complaints. Each one of you has grown into fine young men, and that is the best gift I can get."

"They were bound to," Roy said squeezing the old man's hand. "After all, it's Kaku who has raised them all."

"Who was he?' Alina asked, once they were back at the hotel.

"He was my Sehdav Kaku. He is the one who has raised me," Roy said.

"Raised you?"

"Yes, ever since I can remember, I was an orphan. For me, and a bunch of nine other children, The Malad Children's Orphanage was our home. Kaku was the care-taker of the orphanage and he looked after us well. There was not much to go around, but whatever was there, was made to feel like a lot. Every year, the benefactor of the orphanage sent us our favourite chocolate as our birthday gift. I was the youngest of the children there, and the place closed down after I moved out. But still my gift is delivered to Kaku. I make it a point to go visit him to collect my chocolate, no matter where I am."

Alina ruffled his hair and kissed him on the cheek. Roy felt a bit embarrassed by all the love that had been showered on him; he moved away to pick her luggage, "And now let us hurry up," he declared, "or we will be late for your flight."

The One that Got Away

Babu was pacing up and down the hallway, having difficulty getting rid of his fears. He checked the front window and then the back. And then he opened the drawer to check the motion detector again. Being alone in this jungle was not helping matters. Anyone could come in, bump and bury him in the thickets and no one would ever know. No, he had to get to his killer before he could get to him.

He called his friend Sudhir, a constable at the Powai station and narrated the entire story. "I need to check out the profiles of everyone in the Mumbai force," Babu said.

"But what if he was not a policeman?" Sudhir objected, "Maybe just some freak dressed in a uniform. It's pretty easy to lay hands on one."

"You don't understand. This suspense is killing me. I've got to start somewhere, and you let me know if there is something better in your head..."

Sudhir thought for a while, "You will need to log into Mumbai police's intranet and scan through the profiles one at a time," he said. "But it will not be easy. I can help you with the username and password, but you will still need access to a computer connected to the network. And there are thousands of policemen posted in Mumbai. If you need to scan all the profiles, you would need hours of private access to the computer."

"In that case, we can go at night," Babu was desperate for a solution. "We can even spread this over a couple of nights if that's what it takes. You just get me in and logged on, and then leave. Even if I am caught, I won't mention your name…."

"Won't mention my name? Yes, that is easy…," Sudhir said sarcastically.

"C'mon, you know I am good on my word. Besides, no one will know."

"Well, it's a terrible idea," Sudhir seceded after some persuasion. "But we can't do this in Powai. It will be more difficult to deny everything if it happens here."

"Then, what can we do?"

"Our best bet is the headquarters. I will be able to get you in that building much easier than any other local station. You come down here and meet me near the Vihar society at seven, and then I will take you along."

Babu thanked him and hung up immediately, not giving Sudhir enough time to change his mind.

Alina's Jodhpur flight landed at 1:30 p.m. It was a seventy-five kms ride to the sleeping village of Pali. Once out of the perimeters of the city, Alina was greeted by the sight of the dust, sand and the scorched earth of the desert. She asked the driver to switch off the air conditioner and in spite of his subdued protests, rolled down the windows. The speeding warm air hit her, kissing away all the moisture from her face. She began filtering the sandy images to see if she could place her parents in the middle of this beautiful desert, going through their daily chores – working in the fields, carrying water from the well and sweeping away the sand from the perimeter of the house. Though Alina did not have any recollections of the desert, being here made her feel closer to her parents.

From the moment she entered the village boundaries, Alina had a bunch of semi-naked little children laughing and chasing the car. Alina stuck her head out and waved at them, cheering them on to follow her. Pali was like a poster village straight out of the pages of a Rajasthan tourism catalogue – narrow lanes, single storied houses painted with colourful motifs and the sparse and short thorny trees on either side of the streets. The roads had a bedding of an inch of sand, and the car made a slow churning sound as it rolled across. They reached what looked like the village centre, comprising a well and a tank, constructed adjacent to a huge babul tree.

She held out a piece of paper to the elderly village folk who were crowded around the tree. They held the paper in their hand, turn by turn indicating that they could not read – all the while smiling at Alina with their blackened, crooked teeth. Finally, a young girl of about fifteen took the paper and directed Alina to the scribbled address.

Alina's maternal uncle opened the gates of the house even before the car came to a complete halt. Her uncle's house was a small dwelling – a well-marked courtyard with the holy *tulsi* plant as its centrepiece. The uncle lived alone with his wife; they had two daughters, both happily married in Jaipur and a son from whom they had not heard in the last five years but believed was living somewhere in the Gulf. Alina's uncle and aunt had not seen her since the death of her parents, but were nonetheless elated to welcome her home. They knew nothing about Arun's death, and so Alina had to check her emotions whenever they asked a question, sprinkling her answers with poorly constructed lies she wished were true.

Roy was constantly checking his mobile for messages. He was glad that Alina had reached safely, but was missing her badly as he sat patiently in the doctor's chamber. He had tried to explain to the receptionist that he only needed to meet the doctor for an investigation but she insisted that he take a number and wait in the queue. Roy paid the requisite fees and was directed to the waiting room. From there he was cleared off to another smaller room where he could see a series of red ascending numbers flashing on a signboard. He waited for his number to flash. He missed the days when he could nonchalantly pull out the officer's badge and get things done.

▼

Babu was tentative entering the headquarters and tried to hide his face behind Sudhir as much as possible. The building was almost empty. The peons were cleaning and arranging the desks of the officers and changing into their everyday clothes. Sudhir took him to the office cafeteria and ordered a couple of teas and samosas. He was trying to get into a casual conversation with Babu, but Babu was too nervous to pay attention – staring at the stained tables and rusted chairs, and counting the minutes as they passed by. After spending a good hour in the cafeteria, Sudhir took him to the third floor of the five-storied building. The elevator opened into a long dimly lit passage. As they walked, their footsteps echoed among the semi plastered damp walls of the building. Sudhir reached the toilet at the end of the passageway, and then took a right into another corridor, pausing for a moment to run over directions. After making two more turns and climbing down a small flight of stairs, Sudhir finally stopped outside a small cabin, with its doors ajar.

"Come inside. I have everything ready here," he said, directing Babu to a computer. Sudhir punched in the login id and password. Then he ran some queries in the system and a picture appeared on the screen. "There you go," he said. "Now all you have to do is just keep clicking the mouse. One by one, the pictures and profiles of all the Mumbai policemen will appear on the screen. If you find the one you are looking for, take a print and then we will see what can be done." Babu nodded.

"Whatever happens, lock the computer and get out by five in the morning. If you are not finished by that time, then I will bring you tomorrow again and you can continue the search. You will find some snacks in the lower drawer of the desk. I know how hungry you can get," Sudhir smiled. Babu could only reply with a feeble grin, feeling scared of being alone in the police headquarters.

▼

It was 9 p.m. Alina was relishing the time spent with her uncle and aunt. It was filled with warmth of the nostalgic, innocuous banter that was rare in her life. They kept saying that she had grown thinner and that she should come over more often. She kept politely smiling and promising to visit again. For dinner, she was served the traditional plate of daal-churma and baati, which she ate with her hands while seated on a mat on the floor. Post dinner, Alina casually asked them about Babu's parents and their address in town, but postponed the actual visit until the next day. For now, she was enjoying being with her family.

It was 10 p.m. Ketkar was hating his job. He always hated it when he was made to work. It had been five years since he had been entrusted with the charge of managing a bunch of juniors, and he had taken his managerial responsibilities seriously – ensuring that he delegates as much work as possible. Sometimes he even volunteered to take extra work from the higher ups to pass it on to the juniors. But today was no fun at all. He knew Shantanu was taking a personal interest in the case and would be furious if Ketkar didn't deliver his report on the suicide angle by the following morning. But going through all these files had made him hungry – he felt it would be alright to walk down for some vada paav and cola and then come later to sort the mess.

▼

It was 10:30 p.m. Finally Roy got a chance to meet Dr. Kapoor. The doctor had a well-rounded, calm face with silver spectacles, a beautiful smile and spoke in a disarmingly sweet voice – half of the boxes towards a roaring medical career already checked. "Sorry to keep you waiting," the doctor said. "My secretary told me why you have come, so I kept you till the last so that we can discuss this freely." Roy was not so sure. In his experience, no one wants to assist with a murder inquiry, and perhaps prudently so.

"Alina told me that Arun visited you right before his death. Was it anything serious?" Roy asked.

"No, no nothing at all," Kapoor responded, casually rubbing his eyes beneath the spectacles. "He just had a viral fever. Was running a temperature and feeling cold. We did some blood tests and I recommended the standard medicines."

"I see, and in general, how was he keeping up? Anything to worry about, any signs of depression. Anything which made you take notice?"

"No, nothing at all. He was keeping fine. In fact, he was one of the better patients I had – exercised regularly, conscious about his diet and kept up with all his appointments. I was shocked to read about what happened to him. I have known Arun and Alina for years now. Sad to see these things happening to people one knows."

It was 11:00 p.m. The prospect of entering the dark corridors had been filling up Babu with dread, but he felt he was no longer in a position to control his urge to pee. Tentatively, he peered outside to look for a toilet.

Ketkar felt sleepy even as he climbed the stairs. The cola had hit the spot. He was planning to get his belongings and call it a night, too hypnotized by sleep to care about anything that Shantanu might have to say. The elevator stopped on the third floor. Ketkar saw that the toilet light was switched on. Unless sleep had been playing tricks on his mind, he could have sworn that the light was switched off when he had last passed by. It was consoling to him that apart from him, there was someone else too who was burning the midnight light. Just then, a figure walked out of the toiler door and appeared in the light.

It was not clear to Babu whether it was Ketkar or himself who was the first to see the other. But at that moment, he stood right in front of Ketkar, eye to eye, only ten metres separating the two. And at this most inopportune of all moments, he felt his hands shaking and legs frozen. They remained frozen even as he saw Ketkar charging towards him, his right hand reaching for the holster. Ketkar took out the pistol in a smooth motion and aimed it at Babu. Babu could hear the gun shot even as he ducked, stumbled, picked himself up and stumbled again, hurling himself to the right. He frantically criss-crossed the unwieldy maze of corridors, turning and ducking constantly. Ketkar kept up the pace as much as his body allowed him to, and at the same time hoping that none of the guards had heard the gun shot. Babu eventually found the stairs and dived into them. He kept running, even as the sound of Ketkar's footsteps slowly started to fade away.

Ketkar stood at the end of the passageway, puffing out his breath. He looked helplessly out of the window, not being able to do anything to stop Babu from running out of the building and disappearing into the streets. He was feeling scared. Twice now had he let a petty clerk get away from his grasp, his client was not going to be happy about it. Ketkar dialled his client and narrated the entire episode. The person at the other end hung up without a response.

Babu hurriedly hailed a taxi and got down at the nearest bus station. He immediately fished out Jayesh's card from his purse and dialled the number. The line was busy. He tried again. This time, an irate Jayesh picked up the phone. "Babu, I hope you understand that during this hour, I deal with my clients based in the US," he said. "You really need to have a good reason to be disturbing me...." But he calmed down as soon as he heard Babu's story.

"You have been an idiot," he said. "What was the need to venture out like this all alone? Anyway, right now you go straight to the farmhouse. That is still the safest place that you can be. I will try and use my contacts in the police to find out who he was. If needed, we can get you to log back into the system to go through the profiles...this time with full protection." He hung up. His intuition told him that Babu was the key which could unlock the mystery surrounding Arun's death.

A Mother Speaks

Alina reckoned it was the freshness of the village air that made her wake up with the sun. She got ready and a fresh glass of goat milk later, was out of the door. Her car stopped in front of a single-storied building. The building was expansively spread over a large area, but had quite clearly seen better days. The copper carvings on the door were disjointed at the ends and blue murals covering the outside walls were visible only in patches. The walls were cracked and ant homes had sprung up in between layers of bricks. The entire structure seemed an ode to a lost battle against the relentless sweep of the desert winds.

Gauri, an old lady, part of her face covered by her tattered sari answered the door.

"Hello, I am Alina" she sheepishly introduced herself. "I have come from Mumbai and wanted to speak to you. Can I come in?"

Though Alina, could hardly see Gauri's face, she could sense that the mention of Mumbai evoked a longing on the old lady's face. Gauri signalled Alina in. It was a big courtyard, all but empty save for a single charpoy at the centre. An old gentleman dressed in white overalls and a bright red turban sat there smoking a hookah. Habituated by custom, he got up and went inside the house as soon as he saw an unknown lady entering the house. Alina could see the entrance of the room the elderly gentleman limped into, but because of the pitch darkness pervading the interiors of the house, she could not make out anything inside.

Alina explained to Babu's mother that she was Arun's younger sister, careful not to mention anything about what had happened to him or to Shankar. Gauri spent a couple of moments trying to remind herself who Arun was, and then her confused countenance gave way to a fulfilled toothless smile. She took Alina's hands into hers, and spoke, "So blessed am I that you came to visit me. Tell me, is there something I can do for you?"

"No, I just came to say hello," Alina replied with a sense of guilt. "I had come to visit my uncle. Arun told me about Shankar and Babu and asked me to drop by."

"That is so sweet of him. Arun was always such a nice kid. I can still picture the three running around the house. How is he?"

"He is doing fine," Alina said, trying hard not to think of him.

"And did you happen to meet Shankar and Babu? Any news of them? I have not heard from them for ages," she asked hesitantly, afraid to offend her guest with innocuous questions.

"No, I have never met them. Just heard about them from Arun," Alina replied.

Alina could see the old woman tearing up at the answer. Gauri took the tip of her sari and dabbed it against her eyes.

"It's not your fault dear," she said noticing Alina's concerned face. "The last I heard from Shankar, he told me he was working for Arun. I thought you must have known him."

Babu had never mentioned anything about Shankar working with Arun. "When was that?" Alina asked.

"It was the last time I spoke to him. I don't even recall when. Must be somewhere around fifteen years ago. I stopped counting after five."

"Did he happen to mention what kind of work?"

"No dear. He used to just call, say that he was fine and hang up the phone. He used to get angry if I asked him any questions."

It was clear to Alina that Gauri would not be able to help her any more than she had. She wanted to get up and leave; but she felt sorry for the old lady who had a lot to say, but no one to say it to.

"When you walked in today, I thought you had some news of my sons," she said with a sigh. "But of late I think that the village folk have also realised that my sons are not coming back, so they always take care to be extra sweet to us. The mothers send their kids over to run our small errands and the sweet maker always comes to drop some sweets at my door, even though I tell him I don't have the teeth to eat them anymore," she chuckled for a moment, but then again went grim, as though scolding herself for the sin. "But they can be wicked also, always blaming my children for not coming back. I feel bad, because you know, both of them were nice to me when they were young. Shankar used to steal the best flowers from the neighbour's gardens for me to put in my hair, and Babu used to save his pocket money to buy me bangles. I remember once their father had brought us a game of Ludo from the city, and for an entire year we spent our afternoons playing Ludo. It was the most wonderful time – just the three of us."

A lone tear escaped her graceful control, and rolled down her wrinkled cheek. "And I know that you have not come here so far after all these years just to meet us village folk. I know that you are hiding something from me, but it's just as well that you don't tell me." She looked at the sky, as if asking god to grant her one last wish, "Denial is the only support that lets us count our days. I don't want you to take that away from us." Saying that she got up, indicating the end of the interview. Alina was too overwhelmed to let out any parting greeting. She let herself out of the front gate, turning back just in time to see the old lady getting enveloped by the darkness of the inner house.

Alina landed at the Mumbai airport and took the cab straight to Roy's apartment. Roy had been waiting for her at the door of his building. The cab picked him up, and sprinted towards Lonavala, towards Jayesh's farmhouse.

Alina snugged beside Roy. "Thank you for coming with me." Roy looked at her and smiled. He felt agreeably irritated that he was being thanked for such a pleasant request. "What did the doctor say?" Alina asked.

"He said Arun had been suffering from a mild case of viral fever and nothing else."

"That's strange," Alina said. "You remember how the officers were mentioning his room was very cold. Why would he set the air conditioning to so low a temperature if he was suffering from fever? There must be something that the doctor is hiding from you."

Roy nodded, feigning interest. "So why do you want to meet Babu all of a sudden?" he asked, to change the direction of the conversation more than anything else.

"Probably it's nothing, but his mother told me that Shankar was working with Arun. I want to get this Shankar business clear once and for all." Alina did not say that she felt as though she was under constant surveillance of Gauri's gloomy eyes. By narrating her story, Gauri had placed Alina in her debt and she could break free only after delivering her sons back to her.

Shantanu was at his home, rummaging through his papers when a thick envelope dropped from a heap and into his lap. He recognised the envelope at once; it contained a letter he had written a decade back. He had forgotten all about this letter, but perhaps it was providence that had reminded him of it at a juncture when this document was needed the most. He went over the contents once more, and then with a resolute hand scribbled a couple of paragraphs at the end. Once satisfied, he called out his wife who dutifully hurried in.

Shantanu handed over the envelope to her, giving her detailed instructions of how to handle the letter. Her meek eyes welled up, even as she stood motionless, feebly questioning the need for such a paper after all these years. But her pleading had no effect on Shantanu, whose erect frame towered over his wife as he continued to enumerate the directions.

Alina and Roy gasped at the first sight of the Lonavala farmhouse; powerless to comprehend the severity of the scene that lay in front. The house was completely charred, with the last residues of the fire still burning the rooftop. There were some kids who had been standing by the clearing, gaping at the fire, but ran away as soon as they saw the couple. Roy called out to them but they did not turn back. "Hurry," said Roy. "Those kids will surely bring a crowd to this place. I want to get into the house and study it before the police team arrives."

Roy felt the knob of the main door with the tips of his fingers; it was still hot. He arched back and gave a firm kick to the door. The door gave away with a creaking sound. The inside of the house was murky and filled with thick black smoke. Roy poured some water on to his handkerchief and covered his nose, asking Alina to do the same. Roy and Alina felt the soles of their shoes burning as they made their way inside, ducking and bending around the disintegrated furnishing. Neither of them said a word, but both of them knew what they were looking for. Finally Roy spotted a charred arm dangling from the top of the bed. Roy walked into the room wherein lay Babu's partially burnt body, peacefully spread across the bed.

Five hours earlier

Babu was enjoying a soak at the farm. He had filled up the tub with warm water, poured himself a glass of whiskey and was savouring a cigarette. He cursed himself for leaving the comforts of the house and going snooping around for the assailant. But now that it had been confirmed that the scoundrel was indeed a policeman and Jayesh was on the lookout for him, he knew his days of fright were over. Perhaps he could even persuade Jayesh to appoint him the caretaker of this mansion. The mere thought of it filled him up with giddiness. Never again would he have to leave the confines of his lap of luxury.

It was in the middle of his reverie that he heard the beep of the motion detector. The device had so far been more of a hindrance than a help, going off every now and then, tripped off by a rabbit, a meandering cow or a dog in search of a bone. In normal circumstances, he would have ignored it completely, but today it filled him with dread. Had he been so stupid as to have led the scoundrel right to his doorsteps? No, he had taken great care to ensure that he was not being followed. But of course, one can never be too sure in these matters.

Babu wrapped a towel around him and made his way to the little room housing the security monitors to check the feed from cameras. On the third screen, he saw a black sedan approach the driveway. The windows were rolled up, making it impossible to make out the occupant of the car. The car rolled into the porch and Jayesh stepped out.

Babu breathed a sigh of relief. He hastily put on the best set of clothes he could find and opened the door. Jayesh took a seat on the couch. "Are you alright?" he asked.

"Yes, I am ok," Babu said. "It was a close shave though."

"That's good to hear," Jayesh replied in a cold voice. "You don't worry. I will make sure that your attacker is found and punished. But you should have not ventured out all alone like you did last night. It could have ended in disaster."

Babu nodded apologetically.

"Tell me something," Jayesh continued. "This business between you, Shankar and Arun. What is it all about?"

Babu gulped his spit. “I have told everything to Roy and Alina. Everything I know. You ask them and they will tell you. There is nothing more to add.”

“That is cute,” Jayesh replied. “However, I have come to know of something you kept hidden from them. I want to hear it from you.”

“What do you mean I have kept something hidden?” Babu began to stutter.

Jayesh got up and walked to the bar. He poured two glasses of whiskey, dropped a few cubes of ice into them and stirred the drinks. “See Babu, there is nothing to hide. I know everything. The only reason I ask is that a confession might mitigate the severity of your punishment,” Jayesh said. “Is there anything you want to tell me about your train journey?”

“What train journey? I don’t know what you are talking about?” Babu whispered, too nervous to notice he had been sweating profusely in an air conditioned room.

Jayesh walked around the room with the glasses in his hands. He sat beside Babu, and handed him a glass. “Have a drink. This will refresh your memory.”

Babu obediently took the glass and drank it all up in one gulp. He looked towards Jayesh who was now smiling, but the smile slowly turned into a scorn. Then everything started to become hazy. He felt dizzy and grabbed the sofa to stop himself from falling. His mind was soon flooded by hallucinations – of Pali, of Shankar and of him playing Ludo in the sun. But then he felt a sharp pain in his gut and a burning sensation in his liver. Soon after, he collapsed on the floor – dead.

The True Lies

Roy and Alina waited outside the witness room, while Jayesh sat inside giving his testimony to Romil. Jayesh denied all knowledge of knowing Babu, of allowing him to use his farmhouse and anything related to the mishap. Romil wanted to probe Jayesh further, but felt nervous in the presence of such a powerful man. Jayesh through his curt answers had made it completely clear that Romil was expected to neither question nor debate Jayesh's version of events.

"You look tired," Alina said. "Go and get some rest. This can wait." Alina and Roy had not seen each other for the last couple of days, ever since Babu's body was discovered. She knew that Roy had been running between the laboratory and the farmhouse, going through all evidence, combing every inch of the crime scene and did not want to be disturbed.

"I have a fair idea of what went around in that house that day," Roy said finally. "And I know that it was no accident."

"What makes you say so?" Alina asked.

"The evidence, Alina. Someone in there committed a crime, and tried to deceive us into thinking that it was an accident, but evidences don't lie."

Alina sensed Roy was angry that someone had tried to play him for a fool. She moved closer to him, squeezed his arm and asked him gently, "And what does it tell you?" Roy spoke calmly, perhaps more to himself than to Alina, reviewing his conclusions as he spoke. "Considering the circumstances and timing of the incident, I was more or less sure that the fire was a deliberate act, but I still needed proof to justify my claim," Roy sad.

"Now there is only one way to establish a fire was started intentionally, and that is to locate the agent – the accelerant that was used to start the fire. When I scanned the house, there was an unusually burned patch on the floor next to the sofa set which I suspected to be the point at which the fire started. The liquid that was used to light up the fire had completely burnt away, but traces of it were deposited in the sofa set. By analysing it in the lab, I was able to ascertain the presence of petrol, which confirmed it was an act of arson. The fire indeed was lit up deliberately."

After a short pause, in which he seemed to gather his thoughts, Roy continued, "Now the question was whether Babu was killed by the fire or the fire was started later to destroy the evidence."

"And?"

"Let us imagine that you are the killer. Now, if you have to burn a perfectly healthy man in a fire on the ground floor of a house, what will you have to do?"

"I will have to make sure that he does not run away. I will either tie him up or make sure that he is somehow incapacitated, like by making him unconscious by using a sedative."

"Precisely, only that we did not find either the rope marks or any incapacitating agent used on Babu, which makes it difficult to believe that he would have just been waiting to be burnt." And to drive home the point, Roy added, "Moreover, when a person breathes in smoke, there is a high amount of carbon present in the blood and the lungs of the victim. But Babu's lungs were devoid of any carbon. This means he did not breathe in smoke. He was already dead by the time the fire started."

At that point of time, Roy was an artist describing his painting, peeling off one layer at a time. "Once it was clear that the fire was not the cause of death, my suspicion fell on poisoning. And if he had been poisoned, then it could not have been a slow acting substance like arsenic or something else of the ilk. It had to be a quick agent, something which ensures a fast, and a certain death. We ran the tests and the results confirmed our doubts – he had been given a lethal dose of pure refined cyanide."

Alina was stunned. While she knew that something was amiss as soon as she laid eyes on the burning house, it was only now that the complete import of the situation was sinking in. All this while, she had been distraught that Arun had taken his own life, but now with Shankar's disappearance and Babu's murder, things had taken an unexpected turn. "So, who killed him?" she said in a shivering voice.

"I am still trying to find out. But the wheels are already in motion, and if my hunch is right, it will not be long before we would have solved this piece of the puzzle," Roy said.

"Roy is sitting outside, sir," Romil said to Jayesh. "He says he wants to speak to you. Should I send him in?"

"Yes, yes, please do," Jayesh said, wondering what was so urgent that Roy could not come in later to meet him at the office."

Roy entered the witness room. It was a small cabin and his voice echoed when he spoke. "Hello Jayesh," he said, Babu's death still apparent in his glum voice. "I am sorry for the loss of your house."

"The house is the least of the things I am worried about," Jayesh said. "How is Babu's family doing?"

"Alina had visited his mother a couple of days back. I don't know if the police have informed her. He has a brother too, but he has been missing for a few days."

"I see. The police told me you and Alina were the first to reach the place."

"Yes, we were. Alina had wanted to check on him. The one good thing about it was that we reached before the police team arrived."

"I suppose there is a chance of the fire being accidental?" Jayesh asked, trying to keep his voice uninterested.

Roy closed his eyes, rubbing his forehead. "Frankly, I don't think so. In fact, I am positive that it was a deliberate fire."

Jayesh realised that if Roy was saying this, he must have had strong evidence to back his claim. But he was not unduly worried. There was still nothing to connect him to the fire. But at the same time, he did not want to raise undue suspicion. Jayesh figured it best to get some parts of his story in Roy's confidence to cover his tracks.

"There is something that I want you to know about this fire," Jayesh said. "Well, not exactly about the fire, but I do know something about the events leading up to it."

Roy pulled out his notepad. "I am listening," he said.

"Babu had called me the very night before the fire (true). He said he had run into the assailant who had tried to kidnap him earlier (true). He also mentioned that it was not actually a policeman, but someone just dressed in those clothes (false). I advised him to head straight towards the farmhouse (true). He did make his way to the farmhouse (true), but he kept saying that he had a feeling that there was a car continuously following him (false)." He paused to sense whether Roy was taking the bait. "Quite frankly, I am not bothered about my farmhouse (true), but in a way, I feel responsible for his death (true!). I am sorry for his family (true). Let me know if there is anything I can do to help them."

Roy nodded, but kept quiet. He pulled out a cigarette from the box, and tapped it twice on the table before lighting it up. Roy could immediately see that Jayesh was irritated with the smoke, but he kept puffing the cigarette regardless – a subtle, yet conscious attempt to establish his dominance in the room. "Is it possible that the person who had earlier tried to kidnap Babu stealthily followed him to the farmhouse and then burned him inside?"

"Well, that can be one theory," Jayesh mumbled, glad that Roy was falling for his theory.

"And just for the records, you hadn't seen Babu since the day we left Lonavala?"

"No, of course not," Jayesh answered calmly.

"I think that would be all that....," Roy was stopped mid-sentence by a knock at the door.

"Sorry to bother you guys," Alina said as she entered the room, "But there is something important."

Alina looked at Jayesh, then looked back at Roy, as if asking him whether it would be alright to say this in front of Jayesh. "Yes, go on," Roy said.

"Asif just called. He sounded nervous. He said he has to meet you urgently. And if you don't reach there within the next few minutes, then he'd be in trouble."

Roy got up with a start. "Where was he calling from?"

"From Powai."

"Gosh, I have not brought my bike. I will not be able to make there in time."

"Why don't you take my car," Jayesh said, dangling his keys in front of Roy.

"Are you sure?" Roy said, his hands already half stretched towards the keys.

"Yes, after all you are still conducting the investigation that I hired you for...I hope," Jayesh added after a pause.

The Masks are Off

Asif had been standing outside Roy's building for the past half an hour, with two buckets of quick drying white plaster in his hands. It had been drizzling and Asif was having a hard time shielding both himself and the buckets from the rain. However, his anger dissipated when he saw Roy park a brand new BMW in front of him. "You have become a rich boy," he said with a grin. "I should charge you more from now onwards."

Roy smiled. "No time to waste Asif. Get in quickly. We have to take this car to the shed."

Asif got into the passenger seat, and leaned back, savouring the feel of premium leather. Roy turned the car towards the link road, drove for a few minutes, before parking the car in a desolate garage.

"This ride somewhat makes up for what has otherwise been a miserable day," Asif said, while handing Roy the buckets of plaster.

"Why, what happened?" Roy asked.

"My neighbour died of a sudden heart attack early in the morning," Asif said solemnly.

"But I thought you hated your neighbour."

"Well, I did. And that is the reason I am so angry. He used to irritate me so much."

Asif had assumed that this would have been explanation enough, but after looking at Roy and Alina's blank expressions, he felt obliged to clarify. "By irritating me he made my time go slow. And for a person like me who is on the hit list of both Americans and Chinese, it is always pleasant to stretch my remaining time as much as possible."

"That is indeed sad," Roy said.

"I knew you would understand," Asif said. "And then on top of that, his brother called later to return the money I owed him. I told him without flinching that my mother had suffered a fall in the bathroom and I was in my ancestral village taking care of her. But somehow, they got the word that my mother, rest her soul, has been dead for over twenty years, and so they sent someone to my place to demand the money. I tell you this country is going to the dogs, when we don't even trust the word of our fellow human beings."

Alina was having a hard time keeping her smile in check, but Roy kept his practised straight face. Roy asked Asif to carry the buckets outside. He poured the plaster on the tyre tread marks that Jayesh's car had created at the muddy entrance to the garage. He asked Asif to take a piece of cardboard and keep fanning the plaster to speed up the drying process. Meanwhile, Roy pulled out his bag from the car and fetched out a bunch of full blown photographs. "What are these?" Asif asked.

"These photographs are of the tyre prints we found at the Lonavala farmhouse," Roy said. "The tracks were still fresh, definitely by a car which had been in no earlier than that morning."

"And what is its use?"

"These are for the identification of the tyres," Roy explained. "Just as a person may be identified by his handprints, similarly each tyre has a unique set of prints and hence can be identified by the tracks it leaves behind."

"And you think it belongs to Jayesh's car?" Asif asked.

"Let's just call it a hunch," Roy said. "From my past experience, I can tell these tracks belong to the same model of the car that is driven by Jayesh. But to make sure that it was the exact car, we had to find a way to, well, borrow his car for a while," Roy said smiling.

Roy went to the plastered surface at the entrance of the garage; and delicately removed the now hardened casting and placed it on the ground. He then laid the photographs of the tracks besides the casting and compared the two prints, carefully checking the grooves, the treading and the wear of tyres.

"It's as clear a match as I have ever seen," Roy said finally in a melancholic voice. Alina could not believe her ears, struggling to associate the kind and generous Jayesh with a murder.

Roy, on the other hand, was disappointed more than anything else. He had come to know and respect Jayesh, and a part of him was sorry at the unexpected turn of events. He took the two pieces of plaster, carefully packed them in a bag and handed them over to Asif. "Keep it safe as this can be used as evidence later."

After dropping off Alina and Asif, Roy drove back to Jayesh's office to drop the car. He turned the car into Fox Capital's compound. But instead of the gatekeeper, there stood an erect and smiling Jayesh, ready to give Roy a welcome.

Jayesh stretched out to open the door of the car, "I was anxious," Jayesh said, without a drop of concern in his voice.

"After you left, I sat down and was thinking about what might have happened. First you come to the station to talk to me when you could have spoken to me in my office just fine; and then leave so suddenly...on an apparent emergency. And then I thought how lucky it was that my personal car was handy for you to zip across."

Roy got out of the car awkwardly. He realised that now they were in the territory of obviousness. Both men were aware of which side the other stood. "Thanks for your car," Roy said, hoping to make it a parting remark.

"Glad that I could be of some use," Jayesh said while slowly circling around the car, carefully noting for any signs of tampering. "Why don't you come up for a cup of coffee," Jayesh said as he knelt down to observe the tyres, and almost immediately noticed the white splatters. He rubbed his fingers on the plaster. "These look fresh," he said.

"Yes, there was some construction work near Asif's place," Roy said, the pitch of his voice belying his nervousness.

"How very convenient," Jayesh said. He placed his hand on Roy's shoulder. "Come, your coffee is waiting for you."

This time, Roy had a different perspective of Jayesh's office. The sofas, the paintings and the colours were the same, but instead of opulence, all he saw was the asylum of an old man, counting down his money with no one to share it with. It was then that he realised what Arun would have meant to Jayesh.

"I suppose you are no longer reporting to me," Jayesh said.

Roy did not reply. Instead, he kept on drinking his coffee, letting Jayesh know that he was being superfluous.

"I have led a long life," Jayesh said. "And when I look back, it seems longer because of the extraordinary nature of it. I have tasted the sham of success and the lessons of defeat; earned riches and saw it being burnt; walked across the barren roads with no shoes on my feet and no water in my throat. I have had people mocking me for my failures and have had the pleasure of seeing them being grinded to dust. But there is nothing more heart wrenching than having a person I love being taken away from me."

He looked at Roy. "Because when the journey ends, it is only about the people we have travelled that path with." Jayesh bent forward to let Roy know that what he was going to say was important. "You should know that there are no limits that I shan't cross to avenge my loss."

"Jayesh, you don't have to present your case to me. It is not for me to judge," Roy said dismissively. "Nevertheless, let me tell you that if you break the law, you will find me standing in the opposite corner."

"You seem to be attaching a lot of importance to your abilities," Jayesh said, crushing the sugar cube in his cup. "However, I will not hold it against you. Your confidence is something I like about you. But permit me to say this," he said with a smile. "It is your immaturity that keeps you chained to the laws of the lesser people. Their laws are just guidelines to adhere by when growing up, and impediments to set aside when one has gained strength. For an individual, there are far more important things than letting society dictate your actions for its selfish need to survive."

Roy fixed his eyes upon Jayesh with an intentness which seemed to bring forth whatever he had been hiding within his heart. "It is a pity that you are not where I sit at present," Roy said. "Or you would have seen that I am not looking at a person on a grand path to self-fulfilment, but an old dying man sick with sorrow and drunk with power, trying to impose his judgement on a world which would perhaps be better without him."

Jayesh gently shook his head, hurt by what he had heard. "I am not disappointed at you for disagreeing with me, but because you have been so ordinary." His voice burnt with passion, one which could only be ignited with sincerity of belief. "What are we but stones if we pass by this life doing not what our heart tells us is right. I don't have many years to live now Roy, and if I am to be remembered for my actions, I would prefer people remembering me as a person who gave it all for the ones he loved."

"And they will also remember you as a murderer of the innocent," Roy said as he got up, laying his half-drunk cup of coffee on the side. "In hindsight, I have been more patient with you than I should have been."

Jayesh held out his hand, signalling Roy to wait. He came close and placed his hand on Roy's right shoulder. And when he spoke, he was slow and grave, "Well son, I have not known you as a young boy. And strange as it may be, but whenever I see you, I think of the child you once must have been. I would advise that child to not think of me as foe, but as a friend who will be of immense use to you some day."

Roy was surprised at the efforts Jayesh was making to win his goodwill. Nevertheless, he firmly took Jayesh's hand, removed it from his shoulder and walked out of the office. Chandra watched as an angry Roy strode past his cabin. He picked up his phone and dialled Shantanu's number.

"Yes, Roy was here to meet Jayesh," Chandra said. "No, I don't know what they spoke about; but looking at Roy, it could not have been very friendly."

A Sister Investigates

Alina was annoyed at the television salesperson who kept badgering her to have a look at just one more model. She wanted to be left alone, her eyes fixed on the gates of the coffee shop at the opposite side of the street. This suburban Bandra cafe was the designated spot that the caller had chosen for the meeting.

Alina had taken the precaution of reaching the place a good half an hour ahead of time. Babu's calls were still fresh in mind, and she did not want to take chance with yet another stranger. She circled the cafe building to find a good watching spot, and decided that this electronics showroom suited her perfectly.

At exactly one o'clock, she saw a tall, middle-aged figure get down from an auto. He was carrying an umbrella, so she was unable to see his face clearly. He reached the door of the cafe, shot a glance on either side of the road and then stepped inside. Under different circumstances, she would not have taken the risk of walking into the café alone, but no longer did she have the luxury of letting her better sense dictate her actions. This man had promised some information that could help them solve the case, and the bait was strong enough to entice her in.

Ten minutes later, she was sitting opposite the stranger at the corner most table of the cafe, farthest from the door. "My name is Sudhir," the stranger began. "I am Babu's friend, and a police constable by profession," he said, laying his identity card on the table. Alina picked it up and studied it carefully; she had not looked at a police badge before but tried not to let her inexperience show. She gave the ID back to him, confidently nodding her head to indicate her satisfaction. "It was only today morning that I learnt of his death," he said. "It was not that I was very fond of him, but I know that I was one of his only friends in the city. I view it as my duty to see that there is at least someone who is trying to find out what happened."

"Why don't you go to the police? After all, you are one of them," Alina asked curiously.

"That is not possible. I am afraid that it may be one of the departments involved in his murder," Sudhir said.

"I see," Alina said. "How did you find me?"

"Babu had told me that you and Roy had been helping him out, so I fished your number from the file of one of the other cases our police station has been looking into." Alina did not need any reminding of what that other case was.

"What did you wish to share with me?" she asked.

Sudhir looked around him to make sure they were not being heard, bent forward towards her – to a point that she started to get uncomfortable – and then whispered in her ear, "That night, I had dropped him at the police headquarters, and I never heard from him again."

Alina was quick to connect this piece of information to the policeman who had been trying to kidnap Babu. She took a moment to gather her thoughts. "Can you come with me to the headquarters?" she asked.

"Right now?"

"Yes, right now. There is no need for further delay. If there is anything that can be found out, then it is better that we have a look at it while it is fresh."

Sudhir had not wanted to get involved in this business apart from helping her with the information, but there was a desperation in Alina's gaze which rendered him incapable of refusing. "Okay, I will come," he said.

Within the next thirty minutes, their cab had reached the police headquarters. "It would be best for me to stay in the car." Alina said. "There are a lot of people who know me there, and it would be difficult for you to get any information if someone recognises me."

After dropping Sudhir, Alina asked the driver to take the cab to the nearest ATM. She withdrew a bundle of notes knowing they would come handy. She was back by the time Sudhir returned.

"I have got the address of the policeman who was on watch that night. He stays in Jogeshwari," Sudhir said, handing her the address. "His shift starts at six, so we should find him at home."

"Let's leave right away then." Alina handed the address slip to the cabbie and asked him to drive them to the address as quickly as he could.

The cab came to a halt in a single lane potholed alley. The adjoining building was a double storied decrepit structure with an open balcony running around the length of the first floor. The doorbell was answered by a large pot bellied man, dressed in just a vest and a dhoti. The surprise of finding a beautiful young girl outside his door was evident on his face.

"Are you Constable Shambhu Yadav?" Alina said, taking the lead in conversation.

"Yes, I am," he said, eyeing her from top to bottom.

"We have to speak to you," Alina said, and walked in with authority, without waiting for Shambu's answer. She understood well that it was the implementers of legal authority who were most afraid of people with stronger influence, and she was intent on faking the part of someone higher up on the legal food chain.

The constable, taken aback by her demeanour, rushed back to tidy up the bed for his guests to sit on. He grabbed a makeshift bamboo stool and placed himself at a respectable distance from them.

Alina was straight to the point. "We are conducting an enquiry into the theft of some sensitive documents from the headquarters. We believe that the papers went missing two days earlier, at which time you were on duty. Did you notice anything different happening that night?"

Shambhu was in a fix. He knew that Ketkar sir would not like it if he said anything relating to what happened that night. But at the same time, he did not want to lie in front of these people. "May I ask who I am speaking to?" he asked, trying hard to keep his voice both polite and subservient.

"That is not for you to know or for us to tell," Alina said in a firm voice, even as Sudhir kept gazing out of the door in a desperate attempt to avert Shambu's eyes.

"Please madam, don't ask me this. If I tell you, I will lose my job," he said, helplessness reverberating in his voice."

"I see," Alina said, biting her lips as if in a great confusion. "Let us make a deal. You tell me what you know and I will keep your name away from any official reports."

But it did not have the desired effect on Shambhu, who still cut a sorry figure. "I know how these things go. My name will leak, sooner or later."

Alina was prepared for some resistance. "See Shambhu, you will have to give the full account, whether you like it or not. But since I realise that I am placing you in a difficult position, I give you my word that your name will not leak from my report," she said. "And because my committee is formed outside the purview of the normal channels, I am allowed a bit of leeway in my operations." She proceeded to pull out a bundle of thousand rupee notes. "Take this money as an additional incentive to be cooperative."

In his better judgement, Shambhu would no doubt have realised that everything was not straight with this offer. But the sight of this money, and the sword that had been hanging over him had clouded his senses. He took the bundle and rolled it into the pocket sewn to the inside of his vest.

"Yes, I was on duty that night," he started speaking without need for further prompting. "By 10 p.m., nearly everyone had left office. Only the lights in Mr Ketkar's cabin were still on. They caught my attention for it was very rare for Ketkar sir to stay late in office."

"Then at around 11:15 p.m. I heard a shot being fired from inside the building. I wanted to run back to check what had transpired, but my partner who was on duty with me that night had gone off to sleep in the back of a jeep parked nearby, and I could not have left the front gate unguarded," Shambhu paused for a second to check if Alina wanted to know the name of his partner. He was disappointed when she did not show any interest, and continued his story. "So I called him on his mobile and asked him to run back to the gates."

"As soon as I turned back, I saw a frail figure running towards me from inside the building. I tried to stop him, but he used his momentum to shove me aside and escaped out of the door." Sudhir was about to say something, but Alina signalled him to stay mum. "As soon as my partner came, I ran back to Mr. Ketkar's room to check if he was safe. But instead, I found Mr. Ketkar scrapping the wall, trying to get the bullet out."

"So it was only Mr. Ketkar there. That you are sure of?"

"Yes madam. I was on duty throughout the night and no one else was in office," he said.

"And didn't you ask him what he was doing shooting around in the middle of the night" Alina shouted, unable to keep her calm.

"Yes, I did madam. But he said that the gun had misfired. And warned me not to report this to anyone." Shambhu said defensively. "I know that it was a poor excuse, but I am no one to question a senior officer like him."

'I understand your situation," Alina said, standing up. "You have done well to tell me everything. It is now in your interest that you not utter a single word of what you have said to anyone else." Shambhu nodded, glad that the interrogation had come to an end.

The Haunted Factory

The curtains were drawn and the ashtray was overflowing with cigarette butts. Roy had been lying on his bed, staring at the ceiling the entire evening, ever since Alina gave him the account of what transpired at Shambu's house. He looked at his watch. It was already ten minutes past the scheduled time. Reluctantly, he got up and put on a shirt.

"Did the traffic hold you up?" Alina enquired as Roy entered her room.

"No dear, it's the whole affair with Ketkar that has been sitting on my mind. He was the only one with whom I was close while I was in the police. And to think he turned out to be one of those criminals whom we together worked so hard to put behind bars. It now seems I have been terribly wrong in my judgement of human character," Roy said. "And then there is something else..."

Both Alina and Roy knew what that something else was, but they were cautious of giving that idea life by speaking about it. "There may be a possibility that some foul play was involved in Arun's death. With all these connecting dots going haywire, it no longer looks a simple case of suicide..." Roy said slowly.

Alina merely pursed her lips, trying to calm the upheaval of emotions that was building inside her. "I am exhausted Roy," she finally said. "I no longer know what to believe and whom to trust. Do whatever it takes, but let me have some closure. For once, I want to know with certainty what happened to Arun."

"I will need to once again go into the details of Arun's case. I can no longer rely on things Ketkar told us. Today is Sunday, so he will not be in office. You stay here and I will try and find out how deeply he has been involved in this muck. Tell me something," he said after a thought, "what time did Arun usually have his dinner?"

"Sharp at ten every night. He was particular about his food habits. Why do you ask?"

"Just working on a hunch here; most likely it's nothing. Will tell you if I come across anything," Roy said.

▼

Romil had stayed up the entire night making notes of a serial murder case he thought might prove useful to him later in his career. He woke up late, and was putting out the laundry when his phone rang. He hurriedly dried his hands when he saw the number. "Hello Roy," he said nervously, hesitant whether he needed to apologise for taking his time to pick up the call.

"There was something urgent I needed to check on the case," Roy said. "Are you in office by any chance?"

"No, Roy. It is Sunday, so I thought that I won't go to office..."Romil responded meekly, almost feeling guilty that he stayed home.

"I need a favour from you Romil, if you can spare some time."

"Yes, tell me what do you want?" Romil said, glad to be of some help.

"I have misplaced the photocopies of the case file that Ketkar gave me. Would it be possible for you to let me have a look at the originals? I need them urgently as I have to question somebody at Jayesh's office..."

"Sure Roy," Romil said. "I can reach office in about half an hour. Shall we meet at the cafeteria?"

"Yes, that would be great," Roy said and hung up.

▼

Salim walked out of the abandoned garment factory for a smoke. The wind was chilly, making his cigarette all the more satisfying. The factory had never resumed operations after the great fire that gutted the building three decades ago. Within days of the blaze, some villagers saw the ghosts of dead workers circling around the chimney and since then had kept their distance. The thick grass cover and the burnt façade of the workshop further added to the factory's spookiness.

But Salim wasn't going to let a haunted story scare him away. In his line of work, such an easy assignment was hard to come by; the prisoner was already gagged and chained. No police alert had been sounded and there was no one who would dare cross the factory compound. He was required to just keep a watch and keep him alive. To top it all, the money was unbelievably good.

Salim always envied parents who were able to send their kids to good private schools, and the money from this job would ensure that he could enrol his kids to a good school. Six, seven, eight...he counted on his fingers. It had been eight days since he held guard over his prisoner. It was not long before his client would come to pick him up.

Salim's pleasant thoughts were disturbed by the ruffled sounds from inside the factory. Irritated, Salim dropped his half burnt cigarette and stomped on it twice to crush the spark. "What do you want now, Mr. K?" Salim did not know his prisoner's name, but had gotten used to referring to him as K; inspired by the big 'K' shaped logo on the prisoner's shirt.

K used his head to repeatedly point towards his crotch. With a handkerchief over his mouth, and hands tied behind his back, frantic movements of the neck was the only way through which K could communicate. "Do it in your pants," Salim growled. It was not that Salim had purposely wanted to be cruel to K, but experience taught him that a little terror went a long way in preventing thoughts of an escape. "Or wait, otherwise the place will stink like it did the last time," he grumbled.

Salim walked over to K and ensured that his hands were tightly chained. Then he unfastened the chains at K's feet and made him stand by one strong shove of his hand. K shook his feet to fight off the numbness. "Stand erect, you!" Salim shouted, thrusting his elbows into K's back, and then with a single swift motion pulled down his pants. "There you go honey," Salim said, lightly slapping K's bare buttocks.

K walked over to the far corner of the factory floor, towards the discarded tin barrel that had been his toilet this past week. K turned over his head back to Salim, embarrassed to watch himself discharge bodily functions in such humiliation. Salim saw the despair in K's deep seated eyes, and once more felt the pang of pity he had so often tried to suppress.

"C'mon, I don't have all day," Salim yelled, recovering from his momentary weakness. K turned back and walked towards his seat, but the trousers at the end of his legs restricted K's walk. He came and stood beside Salim, waiting for him to pull up the trousers again.

"What you staring at boy?" Salim said, spitting on K's neck. K did not speak, but kept staring at Salim with a look that conveyed no feeling. It was making Salim nervous.

"Your eyes are mean today boy. Something going on in that pea-sized brain of yours? Don't forget I can do anything I want with you," Salim said, once more slapping K's behind. "Ah, seems you are chilly down there, let's cover up those beauties of yours." He grinned.

Salim bent down and pulled K's trousers up. But as soon as he zipped him up, he felt something cold against his neck. Before Salim could stand, K, with quick deft movements had wrapped the chains of his handcuffs around Salim's neck. Salim's immediate retaliation was to hit K's knees with his fists, but K did not relent. He instead tightened up his grip around the neck. Salim continued to pound K's knees, but it only increased K's resolve to hold on.

It was only after the initial panicked scuffle that Salim remembered the switchblade which had been carefully hidden within the folds of his trousers. He pulled the knife out. K could see the steel glinting at the edge of Salim's fist, but both his hands were around Salim's neck, and there was nothing he could do but close his eyes and brace for Salim's blow. Salim took a heave and plunged his knife deep into K's thigh. K's eyes flinched but he maintained the grip. Salim held the position for a few seconds, gasped for breath and then twisted the knife further inside K's wound. It's not the thrust, but the twist that does the damage, he remembered what was taught on his first day at the job.

Both men had maintained their strength for a minute now, both fighting for their lives. The stream of blood ran profusely along K's trousers and onto Salim's face and neck, forming a dark pool on the floor. K's legs were beginning to feel weak. He knelt down, and then sprawled across the floor, dragging Salim's neck with him. Salim too kept the knife lodged in K's thighs. Both had now passed the point of physical tolerance, and it was only the will to survive which kept them alive.

Salim thought of how much he loved his children and the new dresses and the new school he was going to send them to. On the other hand, K's thoughts were filled with revenge – he could see no further than putting the bullet through the man who was responsible for his misery.

Salim huffed and struggled, his body trying to collect all the air that could pass through his windpipe. His hands and feet were now starting to shiver, as his face turned pale and he struggled to maintain his grip. Slowly, K felt the force of the knife easing on his thigh. Salim's hand first let go of the knife, and then slipped away from K's legs and lay still on the floor. It had not been a battle of wills, but a battle of emotions. And this time, at least, it was revenge that had triumphed love.

The Plot Thickens

Ketkar was dozing in the office when he heard the wrap of knuckles on his swivelling cabin doors. He was pleased to see his friend Roy walk in. "Come in junior," he welcomed him with a smile. "It's been long since we met."

Roy's eyes were exhausted, and his walk was fatigued. He was suffering from the exertion of working without rest or sleep.

"Is everything fine, junior? You don't look yourself today," Ketkar said. Something was not right.

"Yes, I am tired," Roy said. "Over the last two days, I have made fresh enquiries into Arun's case. I have sieved through the evidence, conducted interviews and spent time in the lab. I think I have a new perspective on how things unfolded that night. But before I reach any conclusion, I wanted to go over these things with you."

"Such as?" Ketkar was no longer slumping in his chair. Roy had his full attention.

"I notice you have your fan switched off?" Roy said, veering away from the discussion at hand.

"Yes, what do you think? It's the Mumbai monsoons,"

Ketkar said irritated, "Pretty cold for the fan, don't you think," he said, wishing Roy would come back to the point.

"Yes, I could not agree with you more." Roy said, looking out from the window. "You know, Arun was suffering from viral fever when he died?"

"No, I did not. Does it have to do anything with the...."

"And yet," Roy cut Ketkar short. "And yet, Arun had his air conditioner turned on full blast in this weather."

"That is strange, although I fail to see how this matters," Ketkar said, sounding dismissive.

"It is the small anomalies which give big crimes away." Roy's statement had an accusatory ring to it. He looked at Ketkar, "You know how the time of the death is determined in an autopsy?"

"No, you tell me," Ketkar said.

"Well, it is an art rather than a science. An examiner looks for different things in the body, and then estimates the likely time period at which death must have taken place. In this case, though, it was possible to arrive at a much more definite conclusion. The coroner's report stated that the murder occurred between 3 and 4 a.m., while the neighbours heard the gunshot at 3:45 a.m. – so it was a safe assumption that the murder occurred at 3:45 a.m. sharp. We are lucky to get such a precise timing..."

"I see," Ketkar was nervous, wondering where Roy was leading to.

"I thoroughly scanned the autopsy report, to see how they had arrived at the 3-4 a.m. band," Roy said. "Apparently, the rig mortis was the primary evidence they went by. You know what a rig mortis is?"

"No," Ketkar lied.

"Well, after a person dies, some chemical changes occur inside the human body. As a result of it, after about twelve hours, the body hardens and becomes very stiff. This phenomenon is called rig mortis. The coroner, based on the time at which the rig mortis set in, estimated Arun must have died between 3 to 4 a.m. All of which would have been fine, but then I had the good fortune of laying my hands on the original autopsy report from the office, and found that the photocopy you handed me earlier had two of the pages missing..." Roy could see Ketkar shifting in his chair. "And I found the missing pages had one additional detail about the state of the dead body..."

"I had given them to Romil to be photocopied. You know how careless he can be," Ketkar sheepishly said.

Roy ignored Ketkar's interjection. "In that page, the coroner remarked that he had come across one more piece of data which pointed to the time of death – this was the state of digestion of the food in his body. The stage of decomposition of the food in his stomach indicated Arun had his dinner just one hour before his death. Since on one hand, no one could be sure of the time Arun consumed his food, and on the other hand, the rig mortis and firing of the gun presented a much more concrete set of evidences, the coroner conveniently assumed the murder happened at 3:45 a.m.," Roy rocked his chair backwards. "But Ketkar, didn't you find it strange that if Arun had his dinner one hour prior to death, then this would suggest he ate at 2:30 a.m.?"

"I did in fact find it funny," Ketkar said in defence. "But how would I know what kind of strange habits he kept?"

"If the police had bothered to ask Alina, she would have told them that Arun always had his dinner at 10 p.m. sharp."

"But if that was true, then the murder must have taken place at about 11:00 p.m., then what of the rig mortis and the firing of the gun?" Ketkar said angrily. "You want us all fools to ignore everything else?"

That was one of the rarer times Roy had seen Ketkar losing his temper. "There lies the interesting part," Roy said, keeping his calm. "The dead body begins to stiffen three to four hours after death, and reaches maximum stiffness in twelve hours under normal circumstances. But the decaying of the flesh is delayed in cold environments, and considering how cold Arun's room was at the time of his death, the rigor mortis would have set in considerably later than usual, a fact that was overlooked by the examiner, resulting in an incorrect estimation of the time of death..."

"And the gun shot…?" Ketkar protested meekly.

"Since we have already established that it was unlikely for Arun to have set the air conditioner at its coldest setting that day, then it follows that whoever murdered him, was trying to set the investigation off course by manipulating the time of death. It was the killer who fired another round at 3:45 a.m. thus alerting the neighbours who promptly called the station, thus cementing the time in stone…."

"Aha!" Ketkar interrupted. "But if it was the killer who fired the shot at 3:45 a.m., then it must mean that he was still in the apartment at that time. Then how is it possible that neither the police team, nor the neighbours, nor the cameras capture anyone?"

"Precisely," Roy said, as if expecting this objection. "I thought of the same thing too, and if he was present, then the footage must have been captured in the security cameras.

So I checked the investigation report. It concluded that the analysis of the CCTV footage revealed that no one suspicious was seen either entering or leaving the building on the night of the murder. But then, if there was someone who already was a resident of the building, his movements would not be suspicious. No?"

Ketkar reached out for the glass of water, drinking it in a single gulp. "To clear my suspicions I went and spoke to the security guards of the building," Roy continued. "And imagine my surprise when they told me Jayesh had purchased a flat in the building, which Alina knew nothing about and both you and Jayesh forgot to mention."

"Didn't you know? I was under the impression Jayesh had already told you," Ketkar said feigning surprise. "Anyway, what has that to do with the investigation?"

"Humour me for some time, and I will come to that," Roy said smiling. "Naturally, my interest was piqued about the CCTV tapes, and I requested Romil to show them to me. This was the sequence of entry that took place on the night of the murder. First, Jayesh entered the building at 5 p.m., and then Arun came back from office at 8 p.m., followed by Alina who came in from the lab at 12 a.m."

"What are you driving at?" Ketkar said aggressively.

"I am saying that Arun was murdered. It was Jayesh who murdered him and you have been helping him cover his tracks."

Ketkar laughed nervously, almost faking a chuckle. "I used to have respect for your intelligence, junior. But it seems that spending too many days out of the force have eaten your brains. Why would Jayesh kill Arun?"

"Who knows? Maybe Jayesh saw him as a rival in the firm, maybe Jayesh knew Arun was responsible for the losses that went through Chandra's account?"

"Just to humour you, let us assume that Jayesh did indeed kill Arun. How do you think he went about it?"

Roy tapped the butt of his cigarette twice on Ketkar's desk and lit it up, "This is what I think happened," Roy said. "Jayesh went from his flat to Arun's flat somewhere between 10 and 11 p.m. Obviously he didn't need to force his entry. He simply rang the bell and Arun let him in. He then made Arun sit down on the edge of the bed."

"And Arun simply complied thinking it all to be part of a childish game?" Ketkar interjected.

"Ah, I was almost forgetting that. When I met Jayesh for the first time, I observed he had about a dozen medicine bottles lined up at his side table. I noticed the descriptions on those bottles, many of which contained different types of anaesthetics – drugs used to make patients unconscious before an operation. This raised my suspicion; why would anyone who is not in the medical profession need to keep these anaesthetics at home. So, while he was speaking and assumed I was jotting what he said, I noted down names of all the drugs in my notebook. I got them cross checked with a doctor; and he confirmed all those anaesthetics had one thing common – all of them quickly broke down once inside the body, making their detection in an autopsy impossible. Jayesh either pressed the sedative against his nose or gave it to him through a drink."

This time Ketkar had no objections to offer. "Once unconscious, Arun was made to sit up in the particular position on the bed, and his hands were pressed against the trigger, so that even if Alina was somehow cleared for the murder, it could be proven that Arun committed suicide. It's just about adding layers between oneself and trouble, as our dear friend says," Roy said flicking the ash off the cigarette.

Roy noticed that Ketkar's hands were slowly twitching towards his revolver. Roy in a swift nonchalant movement pulled out his pistol from the back of his trousers and thumped it on Ketkar's desk, holding the butt between his fingers. Ketkar met Roy's eyes, "This is what it has come to?" he mumbled.

Roy continued without responding, "Once Arun was set-up in that position, Jayesh fired the shotgun using a silencer so as to not alert the neighbours. The bullet pellets went straight through Arun's abdomen, killing him on the spot. Jayesh left Arun's body in the same position and shut the door of his room, knowing fully well that Alina will not bother him when she comes in late from the lab. He then added a sedative to Alina's food, which had already been prepared and kept in her room. This is the reason why the police team found her so disoriented that night, further providing them with incriminating evidence to prosecute her. Jayesh then shut the door of the apartment, went up to his flat on the upper floor of the building and waited. Once the clock hit 3:45, he fired another gun from the window of his apartment, thus alerting the neighbours and helping investigators with a time of death that would coincide with Alina's presence."

At this point Ketkar knew Jayesh's game was up. "You seem to have it all figured out," Ketkar said in a firm tone. "Why then come to me? Why tell me all this now? Just to enjoy seeing fear creep onto my face?"

"This is because I noticed something else which I am yet to find any explanation for," Roy said, in an accusatory voice. "I checked the CCTV footage of not only that day, but for the entire week leading up to the murder. And what was interesting is that a couple of days before Arun's murder, an unidentified man entered the building and never went out again. For two whole days, the man never stepped out. The pictures were grainy, so I could not make out the face of that man clearly, but based on what we have, the guards are positive that they don't remember seeing the man before."

Ketkar stood up from the chair, slammed his hands on the desk and yelled, "I have had enough of these fancy theories of yours. I don't have the time or the patience to entertain you anymore. And to think that I was supporting you all this while. You just wait and see how I throw you off the case," he yelled gesturing towards the gate. "And now, get out of my office!"

Roy folded his hands in defiance, and responded calmly, "You can't do anything now. We have testimony of the guard who was on duty that night at the police headquarters. He is ready to certify it was you who tried to kill Babu," Roy knew it would be impossible to turn the guard into a witness, but he recognized that Ketkar was already on the edge and it needed just a push to tip him over.

Ketkar fell back on to his chair with a thump. "So you have come prepared, it seems," he stretched out his hand to take the cigarette from Roy's hand. "We have come a long way, kid – from a couple of rookies in the police with no one to fall back on but each other, to this point, where you sit opposite me and accuse me of being an accessory to man slaughter."

Ketkar took a long drag of the cigarette, blowing the smoke slowly through his nose. "What am I, but a man of temptations, and yes, I did fall prey to them. I was offered a ton of money for what I did, and I took it. And do I feel sorry?

Well, I will not hide behind that word; it is shelter for the coward. I knew what I was getting myself into and did it in spite of the dangers."

Ketkar looked down at his feet, and noticed a slight stain on his shoe. He bent down to wipe it off. "You sit in front of me and accuse me, and I let you," he said, "not because I can't get out of the charges you bring against me, but because I see in you a friend. So there you go, that is all the confession you are getting out of me."

Roy arched forward and took Ketkar's shoulders in his arms, "I don't need your confession Ketkar. I need your help. What is going on? The more I try to understand, the more it complicates. Till now I had been assuming that Jayesh killed Babu to avenge Arun's death, but now I feel I don't know a thing." He shook Ketkar's shoulders as if waking him from a stupor. "Please tell me Ketkar, or I shall never be able to face Alina again."

"You are right, Roy. You don't know anything," Ketkar said. "You might be able to piece together your crime scenes and the time of murder, but the threads of this affair go far beyond what you and I can comprehend. Yes, it is true I have helped Jayesh, and it is true that I have done it for money. But it is also true that Jayesh's cause deserves justice; and I am proud to have played a part in his battle. And if you too knew what that man has gone through, then both of us would be standing on the same side of this table."

"Then stop these games and tell me what it is that I don't know?" Roy pleaded one last time.

"These are not my secrets and I have no right to reveal them," Ketkar said. "But I will tell you this – the last chapter of this story is yet to be written. You don't have to play a part in it; please go home and stay peaceful. You and Alina will be safe; hurting you is the last thing Jayesh would want to do."

"You know better than to ask me to step aside when innocents are dying."

"Not a drop of blood that has been shed is innocent...."

Roy was unable to keep his cool any longer. He got up from the chair, and grabbed Ketkar by his collar, "No innocent blood has been lost, you say? Then what do you say Arun's crime was, and who is the man who walked into the building that day but never came out?"

Ketkar clutched Roy's hands, which were still holding on to his collar, and said in a placid voice, "It was Shankar who walked into the building that day..."

Roy let go of the collar in shock, his head spinning in a desperate attempt to make sense of things. His eyes were darting all over the room, until he covered his face with his palms to comprehend what he had just heard.

"Everything points to just one thing, and yet it cannot be true. This can't be happening," Roy kept repeating to himself. "But the body...," Roy said, as if finding an impossibility, "The body was right there in the open, for everyone to see."

"Seen?" Ketkar asked, "Seen by whom?"

Roy played the entire episode in his mind, and then he staggered back in a moment of realisation, the chair fell as Roy thud against it. "How can you do this? How is it possible?" he yelled. "So many lives you have ended; so many people you have destroyed?" And then remembering that Alina needed to be told, he rushed out of the room, leaving the doors swivelling behind him.

Planning the Hit

It had been two days since K escaped, and he had spent the entire time plotting his revenge. After getting out of the factory, K hobbled his way to the village. He got the wound dressed and jumped onto the next bus to Mumbai.

They say that for the right price, you can get anything in Mumbai; K's quest was to get hold of the man who would do his job without asking questions. K had once been familiar with the dark underbelly of the city. But that city had now changed. The rising real estate prices and the police crackdown had resulted in the crime base shifting out from the southern nerve centres to the suburbs. The contracted men were no longer locals; instead were disillusioned youth who migrated from the northern plains of the country, tempted by promise of power and wealth. They all looked the same, short and lanky, with the skin baked dark from spending much time under the sun. And it is among them that he found his man, Debu.

Debu was one of the the new lads of the batch, but his handler guaranteed he had the nerve to get the job done. However, more than talent, K required confidence. Just a few minutes of Debu's brash talk convinced him that he was indeed the man for the job. K put on a small down payment and finalised the arrangement.

The next morning, K took the fastest train to Pune, stuffing himself with vada paav and lime juice picked up on the way. He got down at the station and made his way to the city jail. The jailer was a stout man; beyond the middle years of his life with a thin grey beard, and a face on which it was difficult to picture a smile. After half an hour of negotiation, a bargain was finally reached. K would pay the jailer ten thousand rupees and in return he would be allowed to spend three hours in the wards of the jail, meeting whoever he wanted. K straightway headed to the section housing the inmates serving life sentences. After having spent his stipulated three hours within the confines of the prison, K headed back to Mumbai, his face glowing with the satisfaction of a man who had got what he sought.

Shantanu was pacing pensively in his room. Chandra hadn't picked his phone; even though Shantanu had called him five times in the past hour. He looked at his watch. There was still a few minutes left before Ketkar and Romil were to come to his office. His phone rang, "What the hell do you think you are doing? I have been calling you incessantly. You should have had the sense to understand it was urgent."

"I am sorry, I was in the gym. They don't allow phones there," Chandra said.

"Next time tell them the commissioner has asked you to; and let them dare refuse," Shantanu roared on the phone.

"Yes, I will," Chandra said apologetically.

"Anyway, I wanted to tell you how disappointed I have been in you. It was foolish of me to have trusted you with this responsibility. Roy called me a few minutes back, and I was shocked that all these things have been going on while you have not had a clue."

"I have been busy with work. And it's not like he informs me every time he steps out." Chandra was getting irritated by the demeaning way in which Shantanu treated him. Chandra had taken up the assignment as a personal favour to Shantanu, but was now regretting his decision. He wanted to give Shantanu a piece of his mind; but it was his good sense which stopped him from getting in the wrong books of the powerful man.

Shantanu heard a knock on his door. "I have to hang up now, and I expect better work in future," he said before disconnecting. "Please come in," he said, as Ketkar and Romil walked in to his cabin.

"Have a seat," Shantanu noticed that Ketkar was not his usual self; his face was hollow, shoulders were drooping and he was uncharacteristically quiet.

"Roy had called a few minutes back..," Shantanu said. Ketkar was horrified to hear the words. He sank his head within his chest as if resigned to his fate. "Roy would not mention much to me, but he thinks that Jayesh is responsible for the murders that took place at Hiranandani and at his Lonavala farmhouse," Shantanu said. "He requested me to question Jayesh. I want your opinion. Do you think we can bring in Jayesh for questioning only on the basis of Roy's words?"

Ketkar was now feeling more hopeful. It seemed Roy had merely directed Shantanu to Jayesh, without filling in the details. And he also knew Shantanu well; the reason he was seeking their opinion meant Shantanu was just looking for an excuse to completely dismiss Roy's suggestion. "Yes, I agree with you sir. Jayesh is a well-known citizen and any action against him without solid evidence will be termed as police brutality," Ketkar said.

"Yes, yes, you are correct," Shantanu quickly agreed. "Roy has been insensitive to the ground situation, going after important people without consulting or keeping us in the loop."

"I am afraid that has been the case sir," Ketkar said. "But I would not deny that his investigations have been useful to us."

"None of us disagree with that," Shantanu said defensively. "But I don't know what shall come out of it eventually. We can't spend valuable hours on a wild goose chase. But at the same time, I don't want to discount any theories. Let us put a man to look into what Roy has to say, so that no one accuses us of laxity later."

"I don't think that would be needed, sir," Ketkar said. "I am already on the job. I will speak to Roy and see what is needed."

Romil watched helplessly as two senior officers he admired were in perfect agreement about what each other was saying. It seemed to him their egos would not accept that Roy did a better job of the investigation.

"No, but I think..."

Shantanu was in the middle of the sentence, when he was cut short by Romil. "Excuse me, sir. I would like to say something." Both Shantanu and Ketkar were surprised that Romil had spoken out of turn. With a mix of curiosity and irritation, Shantanu gestured Romil to continue.

Romil gathered his thoughts and his strength before speaking, "I know I am just a junior member of the team, who does not yet understand how the police machinery runs. And so, I don't speak with the authority of an officer, but with the truth of a witness – one who simply narrates what he sees. And from what I have seen, it disgusts me that instead of being thankful to Roy for assisting us in our investigation, we have been sitting on our backs plotting how not to give him credit. He is on the verge of single-handedly solving two murders; and we, even with the backing of the entire force have merely scratched on the surface. These past weeks, I have heard his story and have had the pleasure of working alongside him in the process of getting to know one of the most tenacious and intelligent officers the force could not hold on to. I have no hesitation in accepting that it shames me to be a part of the same police team which has hastened his exit. I know he was fired; and though I agree some of his actions at that time were illegal, I believe they will stand the test of human and moral standards."

Ketkar looked at Shantanu. But instead of making Romil stop, he found Shantanu intently listening to Romil. This is not going to end well for Romil, he thought.

"All our lives, our moralities are driven to conform to the crowd," Romil continued, "we wait for the school to choose us, for our friends to choose us, for our bosses to like us. We depend on the charity of others to derive happiness; choosing to do what the society demands of us rather than doing the correct thing. But every now and then, someone like Roy comes along. Someone who has the courage to do what we all, deep in our hearts know is right. But instead of lending him a helping hand, we all drag him down to our petty games. And today, sitting in this office with such honourable men as yourselves, Idon't feel proud, but pity for the righteous youth in all of us whose innocent judgement we have suffocated to build our greed on…." Romil abruptly stopped, as if suddenly realising where he was. Though he had stopped talking, his words were still ringing in the room.

Both Romil and Ketkar stared at Shantanu as he got up from his chair. But instead of lashing out at Romil, Shantanu merely looked at each of them in the eye, picked up his coat and walked out of the room. "Was he angry with me?" Romil asked Ketkar, as soon as Shantanu was out of earshot. "I looked at his eyes; they had reddened."

"I have known him for many years Romil and most of them when he was pissed." Ketkar said. "But I will tell you this – those eyes were not red with anger. You seemed to have touched a chord I never knew the old man had."

The Bullets Strike

For once Roy was glad to be stuck in traffic. A few minutes earlier, he had placed a call to Alina asking her to wait for him at the hotel. Roy deliberately emphasised that he had some big news, and she should be prepared – wanting to lessen the impact as much as he could. But still, even the thought of facing her was giving him jitters.

At the other end of the city, K carefully perched himself on the seventh floor of an abandoned, under construction building. With him he carried a bottle of water and a bundle of sandwiches rolled within a crumpled newspaper. Alongside K, Debu was quietly assembling his rifle – once in awhile blowing into the parts to clear them of dust. "You will only get one opportunity," K slowly hummed in his ears, "he will not allow you a second shot."

"Don't worry," Debu said. "I have it covered." Debu's confidence was beginning to irritate K. He wished Debu was more afraid; it is the fear that brings out the best in a man, he had always believed. K took a quick swig from the water bottle and laid it down on the mat, once more considering what he was about to do. Once the bullet left the rifle's barrel, there was no telling how things would unfold.

Roy entered Alina's room and locked the door behind him. He could see the sense of anticipation on her face. He held her hand, and guided her to the sofa, and sat beside her. "Is it good news or bad?" Alina asked even before Roy began. She felt she didn't have the strength to face any more misery.

Roy thought for a moment before he spoke, "It would depend on things that are yet unknown." "What is it?" Alina asked, wiping the sweat off her forehead.

"Let me ask you first..." Roy said. "Who are the people who saw Arun's body after he was dead?"

"Why? Is that important?"

"Yes," Roy said. "I remember you saying that Jayesh was the first to reach your apartment that night. He checked you into the hotel without you going into Arun's room. And then when Arun was cremated post autopsy, then it was again at Jayesh's suggestion that you agreed it would be best for you to not see his body in that state. I am asking, who else saw the body?" Roy was still gently probing and preparing Alina rather than hit her with it all at once.

"Well, I am sure his colleagues in the office must have been there," Alina said, trying not to think much into what Roy was driving at.

"No, Jayesh had refused to grant them permission to leave office citing some urgent work. Now think hard – who else might have seen his body?" Roy had already known the answer to his questions, but he wanted to be sure of it, lest he was hallucinating.

"The police. They would have seen..." without her realising Alina had been slowly stepping away from Roy, afraid to grasp his hints.

"Yes, they did. But none of them had seen Arun before that night and had no way of telling whether he was Arun or not."

"But that is not possible," Alina blurted out citing a loophole. "As part of the procedure, they must have done an official identification of the body. Surely checked the blood sample, and matched them against his medical records and things of that sort?"

"The identification of the body was done by Jayesh. Arun's blood samples and other recognition marks were verified by Ketkar. Ketkar had tried to keep the photocopies of the identification procedure hidden from me." One last time, Roy repeated his question, "Do you know of anyone else who saw Arun's body apart from Jayesh and Ketkar?"

It was as if Alina was finding the room too big to hide in. She began to grow hysterical. "I don't know," she cried, "Somebody must have seen, somebody must have seen." She caught Roy by his arms. "Tell me, who saw?" she shouted, almost angry at herself for having overlooked it earlier.

"There was someone else who came into that building, but never left," Roy said. "Shankar walked in two days before that night and was never found again. I believe it was not Arun's, but Shankar's body that was found in the apartment that night. And Jayesh with Ketkar's help laid out an elaborate trap to hide the truth from everyone else. This way, no one suspected that it was not Arun, but someone else who had been killed."

Alina had prided herself on being able to withstand everything life had thrown at her, but right now she felt tired.

She threw herself on the floor, supporting her body against the wall. Though she could now hope to see her brother again, there was a far serious question chewing her insides. "But if Arun is alive, why hasn't he contacted me?" she asked, hopefully looking at Roy for an answer.

Roy bent down and pressed her face against his chest. "There are many things that I don't know, Alina," he said. "But I am intent on finding out."

Throughout the commute from office, Shantanu was thinking of the case. The moment he had heard of Arun's murder, he had realized that this investigation was going to be special. After all, he knew what others did not and hence was intent on treading carefully. But possibly, he had been too cautious. He was late in realising that Ketkar was not the person who should have been trusted with shadowing Jayesh, but Chandra was not turning out to be any better.

Shantanu dreaded that it was perhaps too late to rectify his mistake. He picked up his mobile and searched for Jayesh's number, but then put the phone away. It was his nervousness which was making him do things he ought not to do. His mind wandered back to what Romil had said. He is still young and passionate, Shantanu thought, not accustomed with the burden of compromises one needs to carry around. It's easy to be an idealist with a clean state; but it's the years which teach one to be understanding. But perhaps it was true that he had been harsh on Roy. He made up his mind to make amends.

His car rolled onto the street that housed his old but comfortable apartment. He looked around for the umbrella but he seemed to have had left it at the office. The rain was gentle and his house was just a short distance from the road. He reckoned he could run the stretch. In any case, his wife would be waiting with a hot cup of coffee to warm up his bones. He stepped out of the car, shutting the door behind him.

Just then Shantanu had a feeling he was being stared at, as though a set of eyes were piercing his back. He turned around and across the road he could see a glinting black object peeping from a partially constructed building. Though the rain made it difficult to spot the barrel of Debu's gun, Shantanu did feel the sharp sting on his right shoulder.

Instead of ducking for cover, Shantanu strangely reached out for the shirt pocket and pulled out his spectacles. He gave the glasses a short jerk and carefully put them on to get a better look at his wound. "Shoot him again," Arun whispered to Debu. This time Debu was more accurate. The bullet pierced through the rain and hit Shantanu right in between his lungs. Shantanu felt as though his very breath had been knocked out. It is the wrong time to die, he thought. His work was still unfinished. But he was thankful for having been shot in the front, through the chest, while in the line of duty – the only respectable way for a police officer to die.

It is said that when one is fatally hurt, his entire life flashes by. But that did not happen with Shantanu. He could only think of two people as he lay there wounded – his wife and Roy.

▼

A chill ran down Roy's spine when Romil informed him of the attempt on Shantanu's life. It was barely hours ago that Roy had told Shantanu of Jayesh's involvement in the twin murders. Could it be that Jayesh had tried to get Shantanu out of the way? Roy decided to go to the hospital and find it out for himself.

The waiting lobby outside Shantanu's ICU was empty. Roy was not surprised; there were very few friends Shantanu would have made in life. But then, behind the continuous beeline of doctors and nurses, he noticed Jayesh's crumpled old figure sitting on a stool at the far corner of the room. Roy went and sat beside him. "What are you doing here?" he said. Jayesh turned towards Roy as if to say something, but then decided against it.

Jayesh kept staring at the floor. "Shantanu is being operated upon," he finally said. "But I don't think he will survive. The doctors have found four bullets inside his body and many of the internal organs have ruptured."

Roy felt sickened to be seated beside Jayesh, but he could not let go of the opportunity to ask a few questions. He kept shaking his leg wondering how much time should be allowed to elapse before it would be considered decent to start making inquiries.

"You seem impatient," Jayesh said.

"You have given me a few things to think about," Roy snapped back.

"Yes, Ketkar told me of the conversation you had with him. Tell me how can I help you?"

Roy found it disgusting that Jayesh could sit there so calmly and offer to help investigating the murders he himself had committed. "I know it was Shankar's body that was cremated by the police." Roy said, pausing for a few seconds to see if he was corrected, and continued on not encountering any protest. "But I still don't know where you have hidden Arun. I know you shifted him to your apartment in the building that night, and was hopeful of getting something from the security cameras, but now I realise you have managed to get the camera footage deleted from the security room computer."

"How much help do you want?" Jayesh smiled mockingly at Roy and said, "I have already helped you with that letter I sent."

Roy remembered the letter well. He was still carrying it in his pocket, trying to locate the sender. "Why would you do that?" Roy asked flummoxed.

It was the sombreness of the hospital that made Jayesh less discreet than he desired. "Initially, I would have been glad if the police held Alina guilty for Arun's murder," Jayesh said. "But then I realised you had fallen for her. By hinting at the alternative possibility of Arun's suicide, I presented you with the only way of saving Alina from arrest."

Roy was unsure of whether to believe what he was hearing. It did not make sense for Jayesh to help him. "You can do all the sweet talk you want," Roy said, "Sooner or later, I will find evidence against you, and whatever you say or do is not going to make me stop."

Just then, one of the nurses approached them. "The operation is over, but he is still in a coma. You two can see him one at a time."

"You go, for it seems your need is greater," Jayesh said calmly.

Hesitantly Roy walked up and peered inside the ICU. Shantanu lay there peacefully, with the many medical instruments speaking in unison of how grievously he had been wounded. The eerie silence pervading the room was disturbed only by the rhythmic beep of the heart rate monitor.

Beside his bed, slumped in a chair sat Shantanu's wife. Her face was more worn out than her age suggested. Undoubtedly she suffered at the hands of the man by whose side she maintains her vigil, thought Roy.

"No one else from the department came?" Shantanu's wife asked.

"No one from the police is here," Roy said embarrassed. "Actually I am not a part of the force myself. I came to ask him a few questions."

Shantanu's wife tried to suppress her displeasure. "You have to wait. He is in no condition to speak," she said, taking pains to state the obvious.

"Well, it would be typical of him to not be of any help even in his last days," Roy instantly regretted his slip of the tongue.

"Who are you?" Shantanu's wife asked angrily, taking care to keep her voice down.

"I am really sorry ma'am, I should not have said that," Roy apologised. "My name is Roy. I am investigating a murder which I think may be related to…."

The name seemed to ring a bell on the woman's face. "You are Roy? Roy Konte? The man who had been dismissed by my husband from the police?"

"Yes ma'am," Roy said, his voice still guilty from the earlier blunder.

"You of all people!" she took a deep breath. "The doctors are not telling me anything yet, but women have the ability to sense what is going around them. I don't think he will make it."

"I will come back later then," Roy said and started to turn.

"Stay!" she commanded; with uncharacteristic firmness. "I have something for you." Roy took a couple of steps towards her in obedience.

"There is something he had wanted me to do if ever he passed away before me," she said. She looked at Shantanu, "I know he will not like it but I can't bear that you think so low of him even in his final hours. You of all people," she repeated. She took a bunch of keys from her purse and handed them to Roy. "These are the keys to our house. You will find a document in the lower most drawer of the living room cabinet. I want you to read it. And if he ever wakes up," she added as an afterthought, "then don't tell him that I broke my promise."

Roy did not know whether he could afford wasting his time on whatever lay waiting in that house; but could not bear disappointing the lady. He thanked her and walked out of the room.

On his way out of hospital, Roy noticed Jayesh pensively rocking his stool, still waiting patiently for his turn.

The Letter

Roy went straight to Shantanu's house. As instructed, he opened the compartment and withdrew what was essentially a bundle of papers arranged neatly from the first page to the last. It did not take long for Roy to recognise it was Shantanu's writing that covered the sheets. He picked up the first page, and began to read:

There are things I know that I have been asked to not reveal, and I am afraid these truths shall perish with me. The last few years I have felt the strength seeping out of my bones. I sleep lighter and feel colder; like a lot of life between my muscles has started to dissipate. Like all of us, I am afraid of death too. But I bear the additional guilt of my secret dying with me. So I have decided to pen down what I know in these papers, with the express instructions that after my death, it will fall upon my wife to use her judgement and do with these papers as she deems fit. In case we both die together in an accident or some other tragedy I fail to foresee, then I request the finder of these papers to pass these on to Mr. Roy Konte, the erstwhile forensics officer of the

Mumbai Crime Branch – for if these papers disappear with me, then it is to him that injustice would be the greatest.

Roy turned to the next page:

In the late 1980s, I was employed as a jailer in the Yerwada Central Jail in Pune. As compared to the plump postings in Mumbai, this job was not particularly sought after and hence I was able to secure my appointment with relative ease. It was not the want of authority that attracted me to the assignment, but the belief that with a little discipline and caring, it would be possible to show a better path for the prisoners to follow. In my years as a jailer, I had set a thumb rule that prisoners could in general be divided in three categories. A quarter of those were essentially nice people who in a moment of madness had done something that they would regret the rest of their lives. I used to keep this lot separate from others; as I knew that if kept in peace, they would lead clean and peaceful lives when set free.

Another quarter was made of the hardened prisoner. Unfortunately these had fallen prey to the harsh realities early in life, and devoted their adulthood getting back at the world. As much as I felt sorry for them, the practical man in me saw little possibility of bringing a change in them. I limited their liberties and entrusted the strictest prison guards to keep a watch on them.

It was the balance half of the population to which I devoted all my time and effort. I was of the belief that these were people who had fallen foul of the law but could be brought back with a little patience and love. I made sure to teach them, to educate them and to impart in them a sense of right and wrong. This system was working well for me and I was relatively happy with the progress I was able to make. But all my rules failed me when in 1989, into the prison walked a man so intelligent and yet so possessed that I was not able to comprehend to which of my categories he belonged. His records said that his name was Viraj Konte, but he insisted he had buried his old life behind and that he should only be called Jayesh.

Roy paused at the mention of Jayesh's real surname. Surely it had to be a coincidence that they both shared the same surname.

Jayesh was a man of few words, yet in his eyes a fire burned so red that the other prisoners were afraid to approach him. But in spite of his tough exterior, there was something hollow in his existence which cried for attention.

He was living a bare existence even by the modest standards of a jail; never asking for extra portions of food, forfeiting his television turns and showing no enthusiasm for sports. In all the years he was there, not once did I see him receiving a letter or a visitor. I felt pity at his loneliness and tried talking to him a number of times to find out what was eating him inside. But every single time, I was met with a deafening and fierce silence.

To keep him occupied, I started giving him small jobs – little vocational things intended to help prisoners better adapt to outside life – and it was here that he truly showed his worth. Within a month in the carpentry section, he was making chairs of the craftsmanship it took others years to achieve. He excelled at the steel workshop and his pottery was the most sought after items for the prison officials. But for all his craftsmanship, his real talent lay somewhere else.

It was the prison teacher who first informed me how good Jayesh was with numbers, and so I began asking him to help me with my accounting and investments. This was his first brush with the world of finance. He began going down to the prison library and devouring entire books on the subjects of stock picking and making sustainable investments. It became a common sight for the prison folk to see him sleeping with the financial papers by his side.

Naturally, my interest in him grew. I started searching for opportunities to talk to him. Initially he never spoke more than politely return my greetings, but slowly he started mellowing down. He began asking me about my family, my friends and of the new developments in the outside world. It was rare to find intelligent company within the prison premises and gradually we started spending more and more time together. But never did I ask, nor did he volunteer to mention even the smallest details of his past. Ignorance and anonymity were the price he had set for his friendship and I always respected those boundaries.

But then one day, two years into his sentence, he asked one of the prison guards to urgently fetch me from my office. This was an unusual request, particularly when coming from him, so I stopped what I was doing and went to his cell at once. I found him sitting in the far corner of his cell, holding a telegram – with his face sullen and full of tears that had been wiped away hurriedly in patches.

"Sir," he said in a heavy voice, "I got this telegram today. It says my mother has died of sickness and old age. Her flesh had been rotting when they found her and hence, they could not wait for me to cremate her." His eyes had the kind of pain which was too great for a man to endure alone; that was the day he told me his story.

"We were two brothers," Jayesh said. "I had lost my father when I was young, and the entire burden of raising us fell on my mother. She did odd jobs – cleaning places, working as a maid, but no matter how hard she tried, we always seemed to have less than needed. When I was twelve, my younger brother ran off to pursue a life of his own and I did not hear from him after that. My mother was crestfallen, but I could see there was some relief too as she now had one mouth less to feed.

"I was always a good student and graduated from college with a decently paying job in one of the government offices. That day my mother counted her meagre savings and treated the entire colony to sweets. I did well in my job and steadily rose up the ranks. My salary increased and after a long time, life seemed kind to us again.

"When I was thirty-two, my mother arranged a match for me. The girl was from Kolhapur, and I fell in

love as soon as I set my sight on her. The next two years were spent in marital bliss as we started to get close, planned our lives of togetherness and over and over repeated our vows of love. Two years into the marriage, I was blessed with a baby boy. It was the most beautiful thing I had ever seen, and often took delight in how small his palms seemed when I placed them against mine." He smiled through his tears at the mere mention of the child.

"But that happiness was short lived," he paused, biting his lips, as if gathering strength to continue speaking. "When my son was two months old, we travelled to Kolhapur by train to attend my sister-in-law's marriage. We were returning by the same route to Mumbai when three youths, no more than twenty, climbed into our compartment. They appeared drunk and were eyeing my wife. She got nervous but I asked her to ignore them and assured her that she was safe in my arms.

At the Koregaon station, I got down to fill up the water bottles. The train whistled and slowly started to roll out of the station. I ran to the gate and lunged in. But as I tried to climb back, one of those boys kicked me hard on my chest. I fell on the platform and the train left without me. I took the next train and rushed back home, only to learn that my wife had been raped and killed on the train. An investigation was launched and from the train records, I found the names, and addresses of the three youths – Arun Ruia, Shankar Kadam Manke and Babu Kadam Manke. I told the police to get hold of them as they were the ones responsible for what happened. But the police were not interested to listen to my story. For them, I was a poor office clerk who was wasting their valuable time. Meanwhile, a local NGO started picketing the police station demanding a quick resolution to the case. One day, when I got back from office, there was a police team waiting for me. They told me I was being arrested for the murder of my wife. My case was assigned to a fast track court, which held me guilty and sentenced me to life imprisonment.

My mother was too old and sad to take proper care of my son, so I put him into an orphanage, the only one that I could afford. My mother made it a point to go and check on him every week to see how he was doing, but now she too is gone," he paused, as if trying to picture his mother's face. "With her not there, I don't know what will become of my child." Jayesh did not break down this time, but looked blankly at me and without batting an eyelid said, "I am going to kill them all. I know not how, but I will kill them all. And I remember the face of the one who kicked me; his will be the last and the most painful of deaths."

Each of the prisoners had a heart wrenching tale to tell; Jayesh was no different. But it had steeled him in a way I had not seen earlier. Looking at his eyes, I knew he was going to do it. I might try to stand in his way or lecture him on morality, but deep inside me I knew he was going to do it – and the world would be too weak to stop him.

The next Sunday, I visited the orphanage that Jayesh had told me about. It was a wretched place with scores *of children crammed into three rooms. I found Jayesh's child in a corner kept in a basket marked 'No 54' with a group of five boys pinching him to make him cry louder.*

I came back home and discussed the situation with my wife. Five years into the marriage, we were still childless, and the mother in her was moved at the child's plight. We liquidated our savings and gathered enough to buy a small house in Malad. Thereafter, we picked ten children from the orphanage, brought them over to the new house and assigned Sehdev, our trusted driver to run the orphanage.

I came back to the prison and gave this news to Jayesh. That was the first time I saw him happy and he hugged me to convey his gratitude. I told him I had taken the liberty to give a Bengali name to the boy. He smiled and asked me the name I had chosen. "Roy," I said.

Roy was suddenly short of breath. He felt as if the room was collapsing on him; and was consumed with an uncontrollable urge to shout. He collapsed on to the floor and continued reading the letter, now much faster.

Every month, while preparing my accounts, Jayesh used to remind me that I was blowing my entire savings on the orphanage and every month I told him how glad I was to do so. Me and my wife could not afford to provide much to the kids except food and shelter, but I made it a point to make them a gift of their favourite chocolate on their birthday.

Jayesh was happy to know Roy was turning out to be a good student. He wanted Roy to lead a life of respect and labour, and asked me to promise him that I would never reveal to Roy who his real father was. I pleaded Jayesh to at least speak to Roy once he was old enough to understand, but Jayesh did not budge. I, on the other hand, was too afraid to face Roy, never knowing what to tell him when he asked why he had been abandoned by his family.

The years rolled by. Jayesh had now spent almost ten years in prison and I was beginning to hope that Roy's love had mellowed Jayesh to a point that he had forgotten about his revenge. But then one day Jayesh came to me with an unusual request. He told me that he was tired of all the number crunching and wanted to work in the laundry for a few months instead. I was disappointed, for I knew how precisely Jayesh had maintained the account books. Plus, it would be difficult to find a capable replacement. I did relent, however, as I did not want to upset him.

The next spring he started with his shifts in the laundry. The task was simple enough: he had to sort out the clothes of prisoners into shirts, trousers and underwear and pack them into separate large bags for the laundry men to collect. But then he began doing something of which I was not aware.

Major repair work was being undertaken in those days within the jail premises in anticipation of a cabinet minister visit, and as a result, a lot of construction material was lying about. Jayesh began to pack these into large bags and pass them on to the laundry men. They in turn used to sell this stuff at throwaway prices and pass on a small cut to Jayesh.

A few of the guards alerted me to this activity, but I completely trusted Jayesh and refused to believe he would resort to stealing just to earn some money. But I was a fool to not understand the larger plan that had been brewing in his head.

From the very day Jayesh started his stint in the laundry, he drastically cut his intake of food. Every morning he used to get up, run for an hour and then refuse anything from the kitchen, save a banana and some lime juice. Needless to say, the effect on his health was drastic. His figure emaciated, cheeks hollowed and the skin tightened around his jaw. I enquired several times as to the reason for taking on such a radical weight reduction regime; but he just smiled and said he wanted to test his physical boundaries. By the end of October, he had lost more than half of his weight and now looking at him, I surmised he could not have weighed more than forty kgs.

The renovation work at the prison was almost over and the construction guys were slowly clearing up equipment and material. That day, when the laundry men came to collect the bags, they found it slightly heavier than usual. Thinking that Jayesh might have packed as much material as he could before the compound was completely cleared, they took the bag and loaded it on the back of the truck. Once the truck was outside the perimeters of the jail, Jayesh used a blade to tear open the bag and climbed out from inside it. When the bus stopped at the next signal, he stealthily hopped out of the truck and disappeared into anonymity.

I had been overseeing the final preparations for the arrival of the minister when the guard assigned to Jayesh's wing came to give me the news. I was shocked at both Jayesh's deceit and stupidity. I was furious at him for having tarnished my record, but my anger was matched only by the sense of brotherhood I felt towards this man who had been my closest companion for the past ten years, whose child I was looking after and whom I knew had been wronged by the judicial system. Jayesh had been in prison for over a decade and knew no one who could help him hide. Surely he would be tracked down and caught.

And then blinded by my love for him, I did something for which to this day I feel guilty of. I instructed the guard to not let anyone else know he had escaped. That afternoon I made a few calls, pulled some strings, agreed to grant favours to some of the most lecherous men I knew, but was finally able to change his records in the official files as having been given an official pardon by the cabinet minister for displaying exemplary conduct, thus giving legitimacy to his escape. This made it official – Jayesh was a free man and he could live his life as he chose, without having to constantly watch over his back.

But in my own eyes I had lost the moral authority to continue in my post, so I resigned and requested the government for a civil post. As a punishment for failing to continue with my duty, I was assigned a starting position in the crime branch – a much junior post than my record merited – and then steadily rose up the ranks.

Meanwhile, I read in the papers of the stupendous success that Jayesh had in his endeavours. I was happy for him, but neither forgave nor forgot his deception. He tried to get in touch with me several times, but each time I refused to see him. The years rolled by swiftly. Jayesh had now become a wealthy man and ran one of the most successful private equity firms in the city. He had resigned to the fact that I was too stubborn to relent and hence had given up on his attempts to get in touch with me.

Roy graduated from the University and was appointed under me in the forensics department. I was ecstatic; there was finally something in my life to make it joyous every day I wake up. But as much as I doted on the boy, I was determined to make a man out of him. I put him under the most gruelling of schedules, gave him the most difficult tasks and watched him flower under my tutelage. Roy showed dogged perseverance and natural intuition; both of which helped him succeed in every challenge that was presented to him. He won many admirers in the department, while making even the more experienced officers insecure of their positions.

It was a few months after he joined that I received a letter from the Home Ministry asking me to join them in Delhi for an advisory position. It was a rare opportunity and would have been a big step for my career. But how could I go when Roy was under my watch in Mumbai, so I refused. My colleagues said I was mad to have declined the position and that I would retire a poor and lonely man, but I couldn't care less. It was in Mumbai that my happiness lay and it was here that I was going to stay. I was also beginning to feel that it was time that I finally forgave Jayesh and made peace with him.

Roy was feeling weighed down by an immense burden of love as he read the letter. He had promised himself that never in his life would he allow himself to be overwhelmed by circumstances, but today his eyes were beginning to moisten.

But then one day it all changed. Roy came to my cabin and confessed that he had tempered with some forensics evidence in order to let an innocent suspect go free, just because he felt it was the right thing to do. I was livid. Ten years back, his father had taken the law in his hands thinking it was the right thing to do; and now Roy stood before me repeating the same thing. I was not going to repeat my mistake; Roy would have to learn the difference between right and wrong the hard way. I fired him from the department.

But Roy was tenacious. Instead of sulking on his setback, he opened his own investigation practise. When I heard about it, I began asking the aggrieved parties to go and seek Roy's help. My wife asks me whether I am justified in doing favours to the son of the man who has wronged me such; and I can only tell her that I don't know. But over the years, the success Roy has achieved has made me proud.

Few days back, I read about Arun's murder in the papers. I was not aware that Jayesh had employed Arun in his firm; but once I read the news, it did not take me long to put two and two together. I also learned that Jayesh had hired Roy as his personal investigator. It was then that I understood that this is going to be Jayesh's final stand. He was not sure whether he would be able to get out of this mess alive, and hiring Roy was his last attempt to connect with his son. I did not want Jayesh to use Roy as a pawn in his game and tried to get him taken off the case. But Jayesh's money had bought enough influence to let Roy continue with the investigation.

I decided I was not going to let Jayesh walk away from another crime and asked Ketkar to tail him night and day. I was desperate for some evidence that could make Jayesh answer for his crimes. It took me a week to figure out I was not going to get any material from Ketkar. Either his mind was not in the case, or worse, he was purposely withholding evidence. So I reached out to Chandra to supply me with as much information as he possibly could, but he too is not proving to be of much use.

The letter abruptly stopped at this point. Roy got up from the floor and ran towards his bike. He drove as fast as he could, swerving it through the traffic and needling it between pedestrians. But he was late. Shantanu's wife was slumped by the pillar at the entrance of the hospital and the ward boys were carrying his body into the funeral van.

Roy went over to the van and pulled the sheet from the body. He held Shantanu's feet, kissed his toes and sobbed over the body of the man who had masked all his goodness behind the shell of stubbornness and sacrificed his life just so that Roy could breathe his own with respect.

A Promise Fulfilled

The morning was kind to Jayesh. He woke up early as had been his custom from the prison days. He got into his track suit and went for a jog. The sun was hidden behind the hills, and his feet thumping the road was the only sound he could hear. Turning around to the Central Avenue, making his way up towards the mountainous incline, Jayesh realised he could no longer sprint the way he was able to when he first moved to this city. His knees were folding up, and he felt his lungs explode inside his chest. Nonetheless, he laboured through the final stretch with the same determination that had kept him running for the past twenty years. Once on top, he surveyed the scene – tall buildings, wide lanes and perfectly lined up Ashok trees. All this had now begun to feel like home. But he knew that once again in life, he would have to leave everything behind. What a grand journey his life had been! And now he was getting ready to write the final pages. Babu and Shankar were already out of the way, and Arun was safely locked up under his command.

But now, sitting on this small stool opposite Shantanu's ICU, that morning had seemed a long while away. His friend was fighting for his life and no victory would be able to ease the pain. From the corner of his eye, Jayesh saw Roy leave the ICU. But he was unable to muster the courage to face Shantanu's wife. Jayesh was no fool to believe in coincidences and he did not need anyone to tell him that his own actions were responsible for what had happened. He took out his mobile from the breast pocket of his coat and once again dialled Salim's number; same result, no answer. It had been two days since Salim was out of touch. Initially Jayesh was not too concerned about it, but now he was getting jittery. Was it possible that Arun had managed to make it past the chains, past an armed Salim and escape? Jayesh decided he needed to go down to Bhose and check it out for himself.

He rushed down to the parking lot and asked the driver for the key. The driver hesitated, offering to drive the car himself. Jayesh asked for the keys again, stretching his hands, making it plain that he was in no mood for a discussion. He got into the car and raced it through the narrow opening in the gate, not waiting for the watchman to open the gates.

▼

It was getting late in the night. Roy filled up a bucket of water and dipped his head in it. He kept his head immersed till his hair was soggy and his nose choked. He kicked aside the bucket, coughing.

Roy did not know how to react. A day ago he was an orphan, and today he had found and lost a messiah, and discovered a murderer for a father. From the hospital, he had rushed straight to Jayesh's office, but had not found him there. Jayesh's driver could not tell him anything but that his employer had driven off in a great hurry. Part of Roy was relieved; for he would not have known what to say to him. But at the same time, Roy knew he simply had to see Jayesh. He could not throw away the only semblance of a family he ever had, as crooked as the branches may be. He picked up the phone and dialled Ketkar's number.

"Yes, he did call me," Ketkar said. "Jayesh told me he was going to check whether Arun had escaped, but his phone has been switched off since."

A chill ran down Roy's spine; kidnapping could now be added to Jayesh's list of offences. "Give me the address."

"It's a discarded factory shed at the far end of Bhose village, about five kilometres from Panchgani," Ketkar said, wondering whether he should have been so charitable with the information, and then hastily added. "But don't go now; it's well past midnight and the roads will not be safe..." But Roy was already on the road before Ketkar could finish the sentence.

At 2:30 a.m., Roy's bike was the only vehicle which disturbed the silence of the Mumbai-Pune highway. Every now and then, the moon hid behind the clouds making it impossible for Roy to see anything outside the circular beam of his headlight. The monsoon wind was also starting to make its presence felt. With one hand still on the handle, Roy tightened the jacket around his chest. It was a two hour ride to Pune and another three hours of climb up the mountain road to Bhose. Roy accelerated his bike. If he had any hope of catching up with Jayesh, then he had to slice his travel time by half. An upturned truck in a ditch by the highway introduced a moment of caution, but was soon forgotten, as his bike zipped past the neon sign boards urging riders to drive safely. Every now and then, Roy felt the vibrations of his phone. He knew who was at the other end, but he was in no mood to answer the call. Roy did not have the strength to tell her that it was his own father who had kidnapped Arun.

▼

Alina had been pensive for the last few hours. Though she was happy to learn Arun was alive, her happiness was quickly replaced by the dread she felt for his safety. She had tried to get in touch with Roy many times, but he had ignored her calls. Her phone rang just when she had thrown it away in disgust. Alina hurriedly picked up the phone expecting Roy's call, but was surprised to see Ketkar's name flashing on the screen. "You should come with me," Ketkar said. "I know where they all are, and that is where you need to be."

▼

As soon as Jayesh stepped out of the car, two stray dogs jumped from the nearby bushes and started barking to announce his presence. He quietly shooed them away wondering whether his cover was already blown. Jayesh glanced towards the factory. The building stood calmly, completely bathed in moonlight with the natural peace which is granted to no other light.

Jayesh tiptoed into the shed as carefully as possible, making sure not to trample the vegetation under his feet. He saw that the shed was empty. As his eyes adjusted to the dim light slowly, he noticed some marks on the floor. Coming closer, he saw a few droplets of blood at the centre. From the spot, there emerged a track through the dust – like that of a body being dragged along the floor.

The track branched out to the back gate of the shed. He followed the markings. They led him into a thicket of bushes and trees. At the end of the track, he found a body loosely covered with branches and leaves. He placed a handkerchief on his nose and removed a branch from the face of the body – popping out of the sockets were Salim's horror stricken eyes staring straight at him. Just then, he felt a big blow on the back of his head. He swivelled around and all that he could make out before losing consciousness was the sight of Arun with a hockey stick in hand.

It took about an hour for Jayesh to regain consciousness. He was tied to the same chair that had been occupied by Arun till a couple of days back. Arun sat on the floor, staring up at him with wide open eyes. "You surprised me," he said. "All this while I was working with you, and I could not recognise you. I took you for an emotional old fool who would leave everything to me when he died. But you surprised me. I think I may have even started to respect you."

Jayesh was in no mood for conversation. He had realised the hopelessness of his situation. He sank his head inside his chest, pondering on where it all went wrong.

Arun felt irritated with the silence. He wanted Jayesh to speak. It was now that Arun felt closest to him. More than an enemy, he was a fellow traveller, who for the past two decades had walked on the opposite side of the same path. They had finally met at the point where there were no disguises and where both stood facing each other, naked of the duplicity which surrounded everyday life.

"You punished me unfairly," Arun said to his prisoner. "Mine was just a mistake of youth. And I have paid its price. Ever since that night, I have lived in terrible horror. How many times I have looked over my back to see whether I was being followed. Every tap on the shoulder, every step in the corridor made me afraid they had come for me."

Arun collapsed back on to the floor, letting the thick layer of dust wrap around him in a warm embrace. "And I have never been able to touch a woman again. I have aged without knowing what love is." He spoke in a voice that had a lifetime of sadness rolled within it. The tears escaped the edges of his eyes and kissed the floor. After having spent so many years living a lie, he felt a sense of closure giving form to his biggest regrets.

Jayesh stared at his nemesis, sprawled on the floor. All these years, he had pursued the idea of vengeance, and now it lay before him all alone and pathetic. For the first time, he saw the human in Arun – a stranger in the world, who had no love, no parents and a sister who was no better than an intruder. Perhaps he did not have to drive a steel knife through his guts; perhaps he had already served his sentence in the prison of life. But no, Jayesh could not let his judgement be clouded by such thoughts. He had to answer his murdered wife and his orphaned son. It was this anger which broke his silence.

"The memories have never left my lips," Jayesh said. "I speak of them because these words have always echoed in my head and deserve to live even after I am gone, if not in my memory, then in yours." Arun curled over his eyes to Jayesh.

"I was in police custody when my wife was buried," Jayesh said. "The court granted me three hours to cremate my wife. The police team led me to an open ground, where she lay alone, peacefully asleep over logs of wood. Rain started pelting down as soon as I approached her. I ran towards the funeral pyre and hugged my wife's body to save her from getting wet. When that failed, I removed my shirt and shielded her from the rain, but to no avail. The fire wouldn't burn, however desperately I tried. After three hours of futility, they dragged me away even as I helplessly watched her half-burnt body getting drenched in the rain.

"I walked away that day, but *she* never walked away from me. I always feel her gaze on me, with a void that cries out for salvation. She was there at the thousand prison windows, she was there within each drop of rain and she was there standing on the other side of every mirror I looked into. She always stands silently, staring at me, with the same question in her eyes."

Arun felt his throat getting dry listening to Jayesh. It was as if a rope was slowly wrapping a noose around his neck. He tightened his fist around the revolver in his back pocket. "Too much of this babble," Arun said, pulling out the gun. "I am not going to make the mistake of keeping you alive for long, as you did with me." He stood erect, towering above his helpless prisoner.

Jayesh's fingers had all the while been working on the knot of the rope, hoping to loosen his fists enough to throw a punch. But now, it all seemed in vain.

It was just then that the first rays of the dim morning sun entered through the ventilation window and lightened up Arun's face. Jayesh turned away and looked outwards at the rising sun. "All is peaceful," his lips murmured. "A beautiful time of the day to die," he said smiling.

Arun stood in front of Jayesh with the pistol in his hands, but his hands were shaking. Two decades back he had committed a crime, and had been living in regret ever since. But this was in self-defence, he convinced himself. He pointed the pistol at Jayesh and pressed the trigger.

Bang! The bullet pierced through Jayesh's left knee, shattering the knee cap.

Jayesh though, kept staring at Arun, not breaking his gaze even to look at the ruptured knee. He had an easy calm on his face – the promise he made to his wife to never stop his pursuit till he lived was going to be fulfilled – by his death. Jayesh had already committed two murders and was happy that he would not have to commit a third. "Finish it off," he said to Arun.

Arun aimed the gun, this time at Jayesh's chest. But he was not able to press the trigger. He felt as if the spoils of his victory were incomplete without the total submission of the vanquished. He wanted Jayesh to look him in the eyes, apologise for his treachery and beg him to spare his life. But well, this will have to do, Arun thought to himself.

Just then, he heard the rustling of the leaves from the outside compound. Arun turned around, pointed his pistol at the gate of the factory shed, and heard the footsteps grow louder and faster, like the echo of an approaching train impossible to get away from.

Roy ran into the shed and now stood at the door facing Arun. Partially hidden by Arun's tall frame sat Jayesh, stooped over his bloodied knee. Jayesh was starting to feel the shock of the bullet and was barely able to keep his eyes from closing.

No words were exchanged between Arun and Roy, as they stood still, guarding and assessing their positions. Roy was hoping that Arun would not fire the gun at him, but did not want to test his limits. Arun meanwhile kept waving his gun at Roy, hoping to frighten him enough to keep him at bay.

Roy slowly started to take a few measured, but nimble steps forward, sweeping away the dusted floor with every drag of his feet. Arun all the while had his gun pointed at Roy, while cautiously moving back. As soon as Arun reached Jayesh, he grabbed him by his hair and banged his head against the chair. Roy froze cold in his tracks.

Arun let out a grin. "I knew this would stop you," he said. "Twenty years I have lived in fear because of this man. And when I finally get a chance to pay back my dues, you come along for the rescue."

Arun again hit Jayesh at the back of the head with the butt of his revolver, and then again. Earlier Arun had felt like a coward in hitting an old man, alone and tied to the chair. But thrashing Jayesh now, in front of his son, had infused Arun's actions with a sense of dignity, and he savoured each blow.

Roy stood and watched while Arun rained blows on his father. He stood and watched as Jayesh's cheeks turned purple and then black, and as all those years spent toiling in the prison began to make their presence felt on his face. He stood and watched as a thin line of blood appeared on Jayesh's forehead, ran all the way to back of his ears and down his neck and began dripping on the floor. He watched the blood pool go wider and deeper until he could watch no more. Up to this point, Roy had been a detective rescuing his client, but that thick pool of liquid had turned him into a son.

He looked up at Jayesh, who had his head bowed and eyes partially closed. They both exchanged a glance – which said, from a father to a son. At this signal, Jayesh gathered up all his remaining strength and kicked Arun hard on the back of his knees using the uninjured leg. Arun stumbled for just a moment, but this was all the time Roy needed to make a dash and land a thick punch on Arun's face.

Arun's revolver dropped from his hand, and he fell on the floor. Roy picked up the revolver and put it in the back pocket of his jeans. He then walked over to Arun and delivered a hard kick to his midriff, and then to his back and his thighs. Kicking Arun seemed to be the only thing he could do. He kicked for the separation from his father, the death of his mother and for Shantanu's murder. He kicked for the cold and the rain, for every lie he had been told and all the misery he had borne. Kicking Arun was the only thing he could do. Roy would never have stopped, if a hand had not tugged at his back and pulled him away.

He turned around. It was Alina who stood there with a questioning look on her face. Few steps behind her, Ketkar quietly stood leaning against the warehouse door. "How could you?" Alina said. "He is my brother." Alina's presence seemed to have had a sobering effect on Roy. He backed away from Arun's crumpled frame, and let Alina step forward to take care of her brother.

Roy walked over to Jayesh and wiped his face with his hands. "Thank you, son," Jayesh said in a weak voice. "Can you please untie my hands? They are hurting me."

"So is he going to get away again, son, while I go back to jail?" Jayesh asked Roy.

"No, I am going to make sure he is put behind bars for Shantanu's murder," Roy said to console Jayesh, even though he knew he did not have any evidence to pin Arun down.

"I see," Jayesh said glumly. "That is how it will be then."

Arun looked at Jayesh. He parted his lips to say something, but then gave him a wide grin instead. "This is how you are going to remember me for rest of your days," he seemed to say, and turned to walk away.

Roy unfastened Jayesh's ropes, and helped him stand. "I am sorry son that you have got a criminal for a father," Jayesh said, and then he hugged Roy tightly, brought his lips close to Roy's ears and whispered, "But you will not have a father who was not able to avenge his dead wife...." Even before Roy could fully grasp what he was saying, Jayesh pulled out the pistol from Roy's back pocket and pushed him onto the floor.

Jayesh aimed the gun at a horror-stricken Arun and fired a shot. The bullet hit Arun on the chest, pierced through his heart and lodged into the back wall. Arun let out a loud gasp and collapsed into the arms of his sister.

Jayesh dropped the pistol and walked out of the warehouse. No longer ashamed to meet the eyes of his wife, he looked up at the heavens and spread out his arms. Jayesh wanted to keep standing there, with the morning sun lighting up his face in its golden light. But with all the strength seeped out of his knees, he slowly stumbled on to the ground and sank into the grass.

Epilogue

Roy took the morning train to Pune. He hailed an auto rickshaw and handed him the slip of paper with the address. The auto led him across a muddy path to the outskirts of the city, and dropped him at the entrance of a big compound. The compound was overrun by weeds and had a double-storied structure standing in the middle. This, Roy was told, was the home in which he was born. Roy did not walk in. Instead, he stood there and lit up a cigarette. Two weeks was all it had taken to turn over a lifetime. He had found both family and love, and had lost them again.

Jayesh had gone through a lengthy trial, and was back in prison serving a life term. He often asked Roy to come and visit him, but Roy was always reluctant to go. He did however, often drop in at Shantanu's house to chat up with his wife and listen to her reminisce of the old days.

Alina no longer wanted to have anything to do with Roy or the city. Once the trial got over, she sold off her Mumbai apartment and moved to Pali to stay with her uncle and aunt. She made it a point to regularly visit and take care of Shankar and Babu's parents.

The police meanwhile instituted an internal inquiry into Ketkar's role in the affair. But the probe team dropped all charges when Ketkar offered to resign and forfeit his retirement payments. At the same time, Romil too quit the police force. He had got disillusioned with the entire system and no amount of prodding by his seniors was able to make him stay back.

Fox Capital was also affected by the affair. The media had a field day covering the most scandalous story to have broken out in the Mumbai financial world. In the wake of the reports, both clients and employees left the firm in droves. And with both Jayesh and Arun gone, Chandra found it difficult to cope with the crisis.

Roy took a step forward, towards the house, but could not muster enough courage to walk in. The rain came unannounced and drenched both him and the cigarette. He threw aside the butt, turned back and walked away from the house.